Undressing
Mercy

Undressing Mercy

DEANNA LEE

APHRODISIA

APHRODISIA BOOKS
www.kensingtonbooks.com

APHRODISIA BOOKS are published by

Kensington Publishing Corp.
850 Third Avenue
New York, NY 10022

ISBN 0-7582-1488-X

First Printing: March 2006

10 9 8 7 6 5 4 3 2 1

Printed in the United States of America

*For my husband, who is the most patient man on Earth.
For my mother, who gave me a typewriter when I told her I
wanted to write and never said it was an impossible dream.
For my sister, who read my work, even when it was bad,
and asked for more.
For my best friend Amy, who is a constant source of support
and inspiration.*

*My thanks to my agent, Jess, who found me and helped me
make my dream come true.*

CHAPTER 1

I'd been seeing Dr. Lesley Price for about eight months; she knew more about me than anyone else on earth, and I resented that. She knew what kept me up at night, and what it took to push the world away. It was her knowledge of me that would help me heal, and for that reason alone I tried to keep my resentment to myself. There are those that say therapy is a relieving experience. It's always left me tied up and out of sorts.

"You're close to your goal."

I nodded, pulled one leg underneath me, and tried to find a spot on the beige wall behind her head to focus on. "Yes, close."

"And the nightmares?"

"None since March." I sighed and finally met Lesley's gaze. "Okay, fine, there have been a few." I frowned and shook my head. "I should've gotten a male therapist."

"You find it easy to lie to a man?"

I chuckled. "What woman doesn't? Come on, how many times have you told a man that size doesn't matter?"

Lesley pursed her lips briefly and then shook her head, brown curls bouncing around as she did. "Okay. But we're off track."

"You started it." I crossed my arms over my breasts. "I'm still not sleeping through the night, and the only reason I'm not checking the doors and windows is because I force myself not to. So when I can't sleep, I lie there and worry about not getting up to check the fucking windows and doors."

"He's not in Boston."

"No, he isn't." I looked around the room, taking in the elegant leather furniture before snuggling into the recliner that I was in. The leather furniture should've made the room seem formal, yet it was soothing and comfortable. Odd. I'd never imagined I would be comfortable in a therapist's office.

"How's your sex life?" She cut right to the chase with that one. But I supposed I deserved it.

"Absent of a cock, small or otherwise." Shrugging, I looked down at my hands. "I just can't find a man that I can get sexually interested in."

"You mean you can't find a man you can dominate in bed, so you don't bother."

I shrugged and then nearly giggled as I imagined myself in a black leather outfit, with whip in hand. "Well, that image has appeal."

"Don't be flippant, Mercy." I glanced up and met her stare. Her face was as serious as her tone had been.

"Fine, weak men turn me off. Strong men . . ." I sucked in a breath.

"Scare you."

"No, I've told you before, I don't fear men or sex. I fear Jeff King, and I'm afraid of him in a way I never thought I was capable of."

"How do you feel about that fear?"

I stood and walked away from the recliner. "Why don't you have a couch?"

Lesley laughed. She had a good strong laugh, and I found her amusement comforting. "It's rather old fashioned. I prefer the recliner."

I glanced toward the sleek leather recliner that I'd just left. "I'm not afraid of sex."

"I believe that you believe that."

I hate psychobabble. Frowning, I looked out the window. "When did you get the new Jag? It's good to see that my money is going to such a good cause."

"Last month." She cleared her throat. "Take a seat, Mercy."

I walked back over to the chair and sat down. "I have a big meeting this afternoon."

"Yes, you mentioned it earlier. Will this meeting further your career with the gallery?"

"I believe so. The Board of Directors will be hard pressed to find a reason not to renew my contract next year."

"It's important to you."

"Success is important to everyone." I drew in a deep breath; my tone had been hard and angry. My next words sounded more like me. "I've never met anyone who enjoyed failure."

"Is your boss still a source of stress for you?"

"He's frustrated, I can see that. I understand that he doesn't want to lose his place at the gallery. It doesn't matter who's sitting in my place, come August he'll be gone anyway."

"You're enjoying watching him squirm."

I flinched and then grimaced. "He uses power to manipulate women."

"His lack of respect for women makes you want to punish him."

Hell, yes, I did want to punish him. "Perhaps."

"Do you view him as someone like the man that raped you?"

"No. He's nothing like Jeff King. Milton Storey is a small-minded man who has no ability to adapt. He's used social standing and the connections he gained through his marriage to keep his position at Holman. It's no longer enough, and now he's grasping trying to stay on top."

"Are there any men in your life that you trust, Mercy?"

"I trust Martin."

"Yes." Lesley sighed. "But Martin Colwell is in New York. He's in your past. You know that."

"Okay, fine. I'm not much on trust these days." I looked up, and she was writing on a legal pad. I hated when she did that, because I was never sure if she was writing a grocery list or creating a psychological profile that would put me in an institution. The timer ending the session dinged gently. I bolted out of the chair. "I'll see you later."

"Mercy."

I sat down and clenched my teeth. "Okay."

Lesley reached out, plucked the timer off the desk, and then dropped it in a desk drawer. "Your work stresses aside, it is important to your continued progress that you address your personal issues."

"I'm here because I want to address my personal issues."

"Yes." She nodded and inclined her head. "Yet you back away when we come close to making progress."

"I try."

"I want you to think about sex, Mercy. Think about sex and its place in your life. Write down what a normal sex life would be to you. Tell me what you enjoyed about sex before you were raped. Did you like it rough?"

I flushed in anger and shame. "How could I possibly want or even think about wanting violent sex?"

"Rough sex is a far cry from rape."

"Yeah."

"Lust can make people want things that are normal when they take place between consenting adults."

"Perhaps." I didn't want to discuss this. I stood. "I need to go."

"Do your homework."

I nodded. "I will."

* * *

Walking into the art gallery twenty minutes later, I felt a little of my past lift away. The work I had done with Holman Gallery had fulfilled me in a way that I had never known before. My world was just fine without a man.

On the gallery's top floor, I found my assistant, Jane Tilwell, hovering near my office door. She was wearing an Armani pantsuit that displayed a slim, athletic figure many women would have cheerfully killed for. She'd cut her honey-brown hair, and I liked the short, spiky do. It gave her a modern and slick edge. Something that jibed, I suppose, with the image she was trying to project. Jane was one of my favorite people.

When I had joined Holman Gallery, I'd realized immediately that Jane Tilwell was being wasted in her current position and that she should be made Assistant Director. That was a situation I had hopes of resolving when I became Director. She offered me that quick and easy smile of hers.

"What's up?" I asked, pausing in front of her and peeking into my office.

"Mr. Storey wants to meet with you before the Montgomery contract discussion." She handed me the folder that held the contract for Shamus Montgomery.

"Where is he?" I asked and glanced at my watch. Frankly, the last thing I wanted to do was chat with Milton Storey once again about the Montgomery contract.

"Mr. Storey is already in the conference room." She jerked her head toward our large conference room, which was on the opposite side of the building from where we stood.

I looked her over and shook my head. "I hate how good you look in that suit."

"I got it on sale." She smiled the smug smile of a woman who'd saved a lot of money.

"You bought an Armani suit on sale and didn't call me?" I glared at her briefly. "That could be grounds for dismissal."

Jane laughed as I went into my office, shoved my purse

into a desk drawer, and picked up my handheld. The important meeting, with Shamus Montgomery himself, was my last one of the day; it was funny how that didn't do anything to put me in a good mood. My office in the art gallery was the second largest on the third floor, and something of a fishbowl. The wall facing out into the bull pen was made entirely of glass. The architect who had designed the building had favored glass, metal, and modern design. I hated him. I would've given my best Gucci purse for a real wall.

The rest of the room was painted off-white, and the furniture blended right in. At first glance, visitors might think the furniture grew right up out of the carpet. I found it unsettling. The bull pen was no different, with lots of glass and steel popping up out of the metal-gray carpet like a garden of metal.

I picked up the file folder that held the Montgomery contract, and a pen. Putting off a confrontation with Milton wouldn't make the meeting or the day go any faster. The men and women working in the bull pen grew quiet as I left my office and walked through the area. There were people in the gallery that supported me, and there were those who didn't. Milton Storey had been the director of the gallery for nearly fifteen years, and the Board's decision to bring me in had ruffled a few feathers among the staff. I knew that in August, when I became Director, I would probably have a few positions to fill.

When I entered the conference room, Milton Storey was talking on his cell phone. I sat down several chairs away from him and dropped the folder on the table in front of me. I'd only been at the gallery six months. I'd spent that six months rearranging and reorganizing the gallery to suit me. Milton had taken most of the changes in silence, yet he'd grown adept at picking his battles.

He ended his call abruptly and turned to me. His face appeared calm, but his eyes betrayed his irritation, and a fear I wanted to ignore but couldn't. Milton Storey was being forced out of a job he loved. He finally spoke. "This contract with Montgomery is a mistake."

"James Brooks wants this contract with Shamus Montgomery. In fact, he made it clear that he has a significant amount of personal interest in this contract succeeding." So much so, that he'd made it clear that losing the Montgomery account could be bad for me. "I realize that he isn't an artist that you would've pursued, but we both know the Board has plans for this gallery that you are unwilling to even consider."

"You don't have my job yet." His face was flushed with anger, but it was the coldness of his eyes that startled me.

I replied, "What do you hate the most about me? My gender, my age, or that the Board no longer chooses to believe that you know what is best for this gallery?"

"I don't like *you*, Ms. Rothell. Your age and gender have nothing to do with it," he snapped and then sat back in his chair. It was the first time I could ever remember him actually admitting that he resented me specifically.

"I was brought to Holman Gallery to do this type of project."

"All you're doing is tearing down a gallery I've spent years building. You've brought in a series of vulgar and profane works that will alienate our clientele."

"Our revenue has doubled in the six months that I've been handling the collections."

"Money earned through thinly disguised pornography."

"If you have a problem with the way things are being done around here, talk to the Board."

I watched his face redden with anger, but he said nothing else. Achieving my failure and dismissal had been number one on his to-do list since the day I'd replaced the young and frankly ill-equipped woman he'd had in the Assistant Director's position.

I wasn't worried about his plotting. I knew what the Board

of Directors wanted, and I was providing it in spades. The door opened, and we were both forced to put smiles on our faces as Jane showed Shamus Montgomery in.

I'd spent three days preparing for my first meeting with Shamus Montgomery. Yet as I set eyes on the man for the first time, I knew I hadn't prepared nearly enough. My grandmother once told me that men are like wine. Some are bitter and hard to swallow, and others lie on your tongue with a full-bodied sweetness that can make your toes curl.

I wondered what he would taste like.

Shamus Montgomery, known for his passionate and erotic sculptures, was one solid and sexy reminder of my empty bed—and he was stripping me bare with his gaze. I returned his brazen inspection with one of my own.

Dark brown skin. Eyes so dark they were nearly black. And a strong and chiseled face any model would love. His hair was shaved close to his head in a style that most black men seemed to prefer. A soft slant to the corner of his eyes reminded me that he had a Chinese grandmother.

I knew a lot about Shamus Montgomery as an artist. However, the need to know more about him as a man surfaced within seconds of seeing him for the first time. There was no mistaking the lust stirring in my body. My physical reaction surprised me. It had been a long time since a man had stirred my sexual interest.

I stood up from my chair and offered him my hand. I sucked in a small breath as my fingers disappeared in his. *Warm, calloused,* and *strong* were the first things I thought about his hand. "It's a pleasure, Mr. Montgomery. Holman is honored to be the first choice for your next show."

There, two whole sentences. I pulled my fingers from his and fought an overwhelming urge to crawl across the conference table and into his lap. I sat down.

I used the time it took Milton to greet Shamus to regain

control. My thoughts had been scattered to the four winds by pure, unadulterated lust.

"I'm here because of you, Ms. Rothell. Your reputation precedes you."

Heat swept over up my face, and that pissed me off. Blushing was not part of the smart, modern-woman image I'd spent more than two years redeveloping. Therapy, self-defense classes, and determination had helped me carve out a place in the world where I felt safe and in control.

Settling back in my seat, I watched Shamus Montgomery pull out the chair directly in front of me. He was tall, at least six feet three inches, and had the grace of a big hunting cat. He sat down in the chair and focused on me as if I were the only person in the room. It was the sort of attention that I had enjoyed from men in the past, but felt uncomfortable with now. God, the man was breathtaking.

I waited until he was settled before speaking. "I understand you have twenty-two pieces ready for the show."

"Yes, but there are always twenty-three. It's what my audience will expect." He inclined his head and fixed his gaze on my face. "I need the right woman for the final piece."

"The gallery will help you find a willing model." I pulled out the contract and set it in front of me. *The right woman.* I fought a frown. Had I just promised to find this gorgeous and amazing man the right woman?

"I've chosen a model."

He's already found the right woman, I thought. *Lucky girl.* As soon as I found out who she was I figured I'd hate her guts. "Good. I've made the changes to the contract that your lawyer insisted on and have included the changes that you had previously agreed to. However, I must admit your breach-of-trust stipulation was a hard sell to the Board."

"I don't like sharing my work with people I can't trust. If exhibiting at Holman Gallery proves to be a pleasurable experience for me, I'll have no need to withdraw my work from your skillful hands." He paused, looked over my face carefully, and then asked softly, "Aren't you interested in knowing who'll pose for me?"

I forced myself to meet his gaze, taking in those dark brown eyes and thick, dark lashes. There was humor in his eyes and in the curve of his firm lips. Again, the desire to know what he tasted like surfaced. I let my gaze slide over the strong, angular features of his face. The man looked like a fallen angel. A profoundly naughty fallen angel.

Smiling back, I looked pointedly at the contract before speaking. "The gallery will secure the model you require for your last piece." I pushed the contract across the table with a pen.

Milton Storey grunted when Shamus picked up the pen and signed both copies with bold, deliberate strokes. He pushed the contract back across the table at me, but didn't lift his fingers when I reached for it. "I'll see you at six P.M."

I looked up and met his gaze, ignoring Milton's intake of breath at the statement.

My mouth dropped open. "Excuse me?"

"You're the model for my last project, Ms. Rothell." He stood as I signed the contracts. "You do know where my studio is?"

I nodded, overwhelmed. With hands that were surprisingly steady, I handed him his copy of the contract, then sat back in my chair. Dimly, I was even slightly proud of the fact that I had remembered to sign the contracts and give him a copy. I watched him fold the contract and then slip it into a pocket inside his jacket.

After a brief exchange with Milton, the damn man walked out, leaving me alone with the contract.

Trying not to shake, I placed it back in the folder with Shamus Montgomery's name on it and stood. "This should be filed."

Not bothering to look at Milton, I left the room and hurried toward my office.

Jane was in my office when I entered. She hopped up from my desk and smiled. "I've answered all of the e-mails in your query folder. You have four meetings tomorrow morning before lunch, and I've confirmed the travel arrangements for Ms. Carol Banks. She'll be here on Friday as scheduled." She walked to stand in front of me and stared. "Well?"

I nodded. "He signed."

"Holy shit, Mercy! That's cool." She took the folder from my now-numb hand. "What's wrong?"

I swallowed hard and shook my head. "You won't believe me."

"Come on, spill it."

"Shamus Montgomery wants me to pose for his final piece for the show."

"Oh. My. God."

Oh my God, indeed. The blasted man had signed the contract after I'd assured him the gallery would secure the model he wanted. He'd backed me into a neat little corner. And it was a fascinating corner to be in. I was both excited and scared. It would've been foolish to deny that I found Shamus Montgomery insanely attractive.

"Mercy, this is awesome."

I turned and glared at her. "Tell me, Jane, exactly what part of this is awesome?"

"Come on! That sexy man wants to strip you naked and sculpt you. What the hell could be better?"

I was thirty pounds past my ideal weight, and pushing a size twelve. I've never been one of those women who dieted obsessively; however, I preferred being slightly slimmer. Also, I had no interest in getting naked for an artist. Shaking my head, I turned to find Jane staring at me. She frowned, walked to my office door, and shut it.

She turned and stared at us with a determined expression. "Mercy, you're a beautiful woman."

"Thanks, Jane." I didn't consider myself unattractive, and I had no way of explaining to Jane what I was really thinking.

"You have a lovely face and a great curvy body." She held out her arms to display the trim, tidy body I secretly envied. "I'm nearly a boy."

Laughing, I shook my head and sat down at my desk. "You don't look like any boy I've ever seen."

Jane leaned against my desk. "Look, a man like Shamus Montgomery doesn't make mistakes. He wants to sculpt *you*, Mercy. Not me and not Miss Perky-Fake-Tits Johnson out there."

I looked through the glass wall and out into the bull pen where Sarah Johnson worked. "You think they're fake?"

"Are you kidding? They can't be anything else," Jane snorted. "I've considered reporting her to the EPA."

"For what?"

Jane shrugged. "There is no way she's still biodegradable."

I laughed and looked back to Sarah; Milton was holding court at her desk. I personally found him tedious on most occasions, but it was obvious why Sarah feigned interest. She believed that he could help her get somewhere in the art world. Despite his upcoming forced retirement from Holman Gallery, Milton Storey did have influence.

Milton finished preening for the environmental hazard and started toward my office. "You'd better scoot," I said to Jane, "or he'll have a chance to ask you why you still haven't gone out with his son."

Jane grimaced and darted past Milton just as he entered the room. The sudden movement confused him for a moment, and his gaze jerked from her exiting form and to me several times before he settled on my face.

"What can I do for you, Milton?"

"I was just telling Sarah about the deal with Shamus Mont-gomery. She'd be willing to take your place as a model." Milton tucked his hands into his pants pockets and inclined his head. "She's young and thin."

Young, thin, and plastic. I glanced toward Sarah and knew exactly what was on her mind. It would be a cold day in hell before I'd let her parade around in all of her manmade glory for Shamus Montgomery. I wasn't exactly convinced I could pose for him, but I knew I couldn't allow her to do it either. "Mr. Montgomery made his choice. I did promise the man the gallery would secure the model he wanted." I leaned back in my chair, and watched Milton fidget.

Finally he looked out at Sarah and shrugged.

Miss Perky Tits glared at me and went back to her work.

My phone rang. Milton strolled out of my office, leaving the door open, which I hated. As I picked up the phone, Jane was at the door, gently pulling it closed. I was going to miss her when I went to prison for killing Milton.

"Hello."

"Ms. Rothell."

Shamus Montgomery. His voice was smooth and cultured, yet it woke something wild and nearly unspeakable in me. I wanted to be angry with him for his presumption. The truth was that I enjoyed his arrogance so much that I couldn't wait to tangle with him again. The fact that he'd had called me so soon led me to believe that maybe he felt the same way.

"Mr. Montgomery. I'm glad you called. You didn't give me much time to consider your offer." My opening volley was met with a brief silence.

"It wasn't an offer."

Looking down at my desk, I sighed and then glanced out at Jane in the bull pen. She held up a piece of paper with SHAMUS MONTGOMERY IS A GOD written on it in big red let-ters. I glared at her and turned in my chair so I didn't have to see her or her stupid sign.

"I can assure you there are scores of women who would happily strip naked and pose for you. I just don't happen to be one of them." That was a damn lie. Well, it was a half-lie. I could easily see myself getting naked with Shamus Montgomery; it was the posing part that put me off. I focused on one of my fingernails and frowned at the cuticle. It was a prime example of how I felt inside: ragged.

"I have a feeling that it's time you did something different," he said.

"I'm not stagnating," I snapped and then frowned, realizing that he hadn't said anything like that.

His silence wasn't comforting. I could almost hear the wheels turning in his head as he considered what my response had revealed. Closing my eyes, I waited for him to say something. Anything.

"Don't be late, Mercy."

He hung up. I crossed my legs at the knee and tried to ignore the dampness in my panties and the gentle throb of my clit. Anger and want twisted in my body, and having no outlet for either left me frustrated and thoroughly confused. I couldn't even remember the last time I'd met a man that stirred my body as Shamus Montgomery did.

I turned in my chair and stared at Jane pretending to be working on her computer. Glancing at my own monitor, I noticed that my instant messenger was flashing. I clicked on the window, and I saw a message from Jane.

"Only an idiot would turn down the chance to spend the summer NAKED with Shamus Montgomery."

"Bite me," I responded and then cut off the messenger.

I watched Jane giggle for a moment, and then swiveled my chair to look out the window. She was right. Shamus Montgomery was a sexy and talented man, and women traveled thousands of miles to pose for him. I should feel honored that he wanted me in his studio. He was a powerful artist, and I knew what he could draw out of a woman. Still, his desire to capture my soul wasn't a comforting one.

Exposing myself to a man like Shamus was a far bigger step than anything my therapist and I had worked on. The thought of being vulnerable was an unbearable one. I'd tried so hard to put my experience in New York behind me, but that didn't mean I was ready to go on display.

Despite all of those fears and the anger that he'd outmaneuvered me, I was left with a fine layer of arousal that simmered under my skin. I could almost feel his hands moving over my body, the pressure of his body against mine, and the blunt tip of his cock pushing into my emptiness.

I lowered my head to my desk. "What a fucking nightmare."

After work, I hurried home to hide in my apartment. I'd lived in Boston two years and had used that time to create a space that was unique and mine. The apartment had four rooms, including the kitchen and the large bathroom. My furniture was modern without being uncomfortable, and I'd used a crème foundation color for each room. Then, when the mood struck, I'd bought outrageously colorful pillows and rugs and strewn them throughout every room. I could admit to myself that my apartment was my sanctuary from the world. I'd learned the hard way just how cruel life could be.

I toed off my shoes and left them near the door. After quickly sorting the mail and tossing all of the junk, I took the rest to the kitchen table and sat down.

The first envelope was from New York, with my exboyfriend Martin's return address on it. My relationship with Martin was one of the few in my life that had returned to a friendship after the sex was over. It looked like a wedding invitation. It was. I frowned as I read over the details and then dropped it onto the table. I knew I wouldn't go. Going to

New York, even for the wedding of a friend, was completely impossible for me.

The wedding invitation had unsettled me, and I knew why. It was selfish and terribly cruel, but I regretted that Martin had found someone to share his life with. Though he certainly deserved it. Martin was the best man I'd ever known. A very selfish part of me wanted him to be waiting in the wings for me. Disgusted with myself, I rubbed my face briskly.

I stood up, made myself a sandwich, and brought it back to the table. Then I opened the rest of my mail until all I had left was a large manila envelope from the museum I had worked for in New York. With dread, I opened it and spilled the contents out onto the table. I didn't remember signing up for the museum's mailing list with my home address, but I must have. It was a foolish error. The glossy advertisements slipped across each other as I picked up a press release with a photo of Jeff King's face on it. He'd been promoted and now held the position I'd left more than two years ago.

God, I hated him. I wondered if there would ever be a day I could look at his face and not feel his hands biting into me. I could almost smell his cologne. It made me furious that even his picture had the ability to invade and hurt me.

The phone rang as I choked down the rest of my sandwich. I jumped on it immediately, relieved. "Hello?"

"Hey. What are you wearing to Montgomery's tonight? Did you pick out matching underwear? Wear that great perfume we bought at the mall last week, the one named after that singer." Jane paused briefly. "Hey, are you there?"

"Yes. I'm going to wear my blue sundress, and I planned on putting on matching underwear and no perfume."

"Oh, come on, Mercy!"

"Jane, it is not my aim to seduce or in any other way provoke Shamus Montgomery." I glanced around the kitchen and then briefly to the mail I'd abandoned on the table.

"If you don't get laid soon, I'll have to renew my subscription to *Penthouse Forum*."

I laughed, amused by her petulant tone. "Why don't *you* run out and get laid? Hell, get laid for me, too."

Jane snorted and then sighed deeply. "Men suck, Mercy. I might start going to gay bars, try to find a gay male friend and a lesbian lover. Then I can pretend I'm on some sexy cable show and not worry about tedious things like real life."

I leaned on the counter. "You and I both know that you aren't going to give up men. However, a wild night with a woman would broaden your horizons."

She laughed and I could almost see her shrug. For all of her bravado and charm, Jane was fairly tame, and I doubted that she would allow herself to be with another woman. She chattered for another few minutes and reminded me again to wear perfume, and then we ended the call. I valued Jane. Female friends had always been a rarity in my life, but that didn't mean I was going to douse myself in scent.

I put the phone back on its base and walked back to the table. Jeff King's handsome, cruel face stared back up at me. Grimacing, I picked up the photo and tore it down the middle. He was nothing to me. I had to believe that. I'd left him and that life behind.

At 4:30 P.M., I forced myself into the shower. Under the cool water of the massaging showerhead, I tried in vain to clear my mind. The truth was, as fascinating and sexy as Shamus Montgomery was, I knew that he was far too dangerous to get involved with. He wasn't the sort of danger that scarred and damaged, but the kind of danger that made blood boil and flesh heat with impatient passion.

Leaning against the tile wall of my shower stall, I pulled the massaging showerhead from its hook. I rinsed the soap from my body casually, and then slipped the pulsating head between my legs. The cool water rushed against the heat of my pussy, making my clit throb with the sweet pain of sexual arousal. With my thumb, I changed the setting on the shower-head and pressed it more firmly against my labia. The water beat against my clit as I carefully started to move the head around.

Would Shamus be the kind of man who enjoyed a woman's pleasure as much as his own? Would his hands move over skin with knowledge and skill? I pressed against the wall with all of my strength and shuddered against the rushing water on my clit. I imagined a tongue moving over me, dipping into my pussy, and then moving up to tease and brush over my clit. The dangerous and stimulating pleasure of teeth grazing and then firm lips sucking.

Eyes closed. Legs stiffened. I came. The orgasm swept over my clit. My insides clenched and tightened in response. The emptiness of my womb was harsh against my body's response to the incessant push of water. Had it been so long since a man had filled me? I wanted a man, and I wasn't foolish enough to believe that any man would do. I wanted Shamus. Momentarily weak, I put the nozzle back on the hook and sucked in a deep breath.

The edge was off. The burning lust that I'd been pushing aside since I'd set eyes on Shamus Montgomery had dissi-pated, but I wondered how long that state would last. I had a feeling that masturbation wouldn't be a permanent substitute for him.

I was half-dressed when the phone rang. By the time I reached for the receiver, the answering machine had already picked up. Pausing, I waited while the electronic version of me told the caller I wasn't available. The beep came, and all I heard was silence. Then the caller hung up with a gentle click. I sucked in a breath, irritated at the fear that slipped over me.

Though it had been nearly fourteen months since Jeff had last called me, whenever I got a hang-up on my answering machine, my first thought was that it was him. I picked up the phone and checked the caller ID. The call showed up as an "unknown number." I hung up the phone and stood for a few seconds, fighting with paranoia and self-hatred. I hated myself for allowing Jeff King a place in my mind. Finally, I went back to my bedroom to finish dressing.

When I couldn't stall any longer, I gave in and gathered my purse and keys. I didn't want to be late; it would give Shamus the upper hand.

CHAPTER 2

I sat in the car in front of his studio, a brownstone in down-town Boston. My fingers curled tightly around the steering wheel. Lowering my head, I wallowed in self-pity for a few minutes, then pried my fingers from the wheel and picked up my purse. I dragged myself out of the car and hoped that my displeasure was obvious.

Shamus Montgomery's studio space was on the entire second floor of a three-story building. The top floor was his living quarters, although rumor had it that very few people got an invitation into his personal space. I knew no one who had gotten that close to the elusive Mr. Montgomery. The first floor was a show space and one of the most popular small galleries in the area.

Pushing the door open, I stepped inside.

Shamus was standing with a customer in front of a large oak sculpture of two figures that were both obviously female. The pose was intimate and sensual in a way that made my stomach tighten. The customer was running her hands over the smooth and seductive wooden sculpture as if she couldn't help herself. I knew that she wouldn't leave without buying it; just watching her fondle it made me want to purchase it myself. Cringing, I remembered the hole in my savings due to the purchase of one his other works about six months before at auction.

Finding the woman's fascination with the piece unsettling, I turned to look at the rest of the gallery. A large stone sculpture dominated the floor space; it was marked SOLD. The lines of the female figure were gentle and passionate. I wondered who Shamus had used for the work, and if she was still in his life.

Before long I heard the murmur of voices and steps on the wooden floor, and then the jingle of the tiny bells over the top of the door indicated the customer had left. Glancing toward Shamus, I watched him lock the door and twist the blinds closed. We were alone.

"You look worried, Mercy."

I cleared my throat. "Mr. Montgomery, I'd like to talk to you about securing another model."

"Only you will do." He walked to the staircase and unhooked the chain holding the PRIVACY sign. It knocked against the wall briefly, but echoed ominously throughout the empty gallery. "My studio is upstairs."

"Why me?"

"Maybe it's because of your stunningly beautiful face."

"Maybe that isn't good enough." I held myself still, resisting the urge to run my fingers through my hair. I hated being nervous.

"You inspire me."

Well, what the hell could I say after that? *I* inspired him, and a feeling of giddy, girlish delight swept through me. I stomped down my ego and pressed my lips together. He'd knocked the wind out of my sails, and I could only assume that had been exactly what he wanted.

What did he want from me? Fighting the urge to run away, I hurried past him and up the stairs. Shamus Montgomery seemed too much for me. All of my thoughts about challenging him had fallen by the wayside. In his studio, a large slab of alabaster sat on a drop cloth in the open work space. A low platform covered with another cloth stood in front of the alabaster. I turned toward the stairs and looked back at him. He stood on the top step, watching me.

"Should we get started?" Had I actually asked that?

He smiled at my question, amused, I could only assume, by the squeaky way the question had come out of my mouth. "Yes, I believe we should."

I swallowed hard and tried to ignore the way his dark gaze slid over my body.

His skin was a milk chocolate brown that made me want to lick him. Regretting that thought, I moved around to the platform and then looked at the large piece of stone that sat behind it. "You don't usually make a habit of using alabaster."

"There've been few women that model for me who fit that medium," Shamus admitted as he closed the door, sealing us in.

"I see."

He motioned toward a dressing screen in one corner. "You'll find a robe behind the screen. Just the robe."

I nodded and walked toward the screen. *Just the robe.*

The robe was made of dark blue silk and smelled gently of fabric softener. I shed my clothes with shaking hands and pulled it on. The silk was cool and fell around me gently. I double knotted the belt—my safety knot—but finally had to leave the protection of the screened area.

I saw a cotton-covered pillow now lay on the platform. It was large enough so that I would be able to lie on it.

Shamus eyed me, his gaze moved from my feet upward until he encountered my face. His mouth curved in a small smile.

"You like making women nervous?" I asked.

He raised an eyebrow. "Do I make you nervous?"

Glaring at him, I walked toward the platform, fuming. He knew exactly what he was doing to me. "How do you want me?"

"On your back, screaming my name, but for now we'll work on the position for the piece."

On my back, screaming his name. I swallowed hard and took a step back from the platform. It was the first time he'd expressed sexual interest me, and, as interested as I was in getting to him in that way, his admission was startling. The blunt verbal admission of our obviously mutual attraction had shaken me loose of all of my previous nervousness and introduced a new kind. This man was no longer just a man who wanted me to pose for him naked.

Shamus Montgomery was now a man who wanted to get me naked for a sexual purpose. A purpose I might've enjoyed under different circumstances. But I had no control in this situation.

My trembling fingers lingered on the belt of the robe. The double knot wasn't enough. "I can't."

I glanced up and looked at his face.

He was staring at me in confusion. "Are you afraid of me?"

The question, so softly asked, was like a blade on my skin. It was difficult to understand how words could pierce so deeply, and so fast. I didn't fear him, at least not physically. However, emotionally, he represented a world of sensuality and pleasure that I'd had long denied myself.

Shamus Montgomery was everything that I once looked for in a man: strong, intelligent, arrogant, talented, and thoroughly sexy. His easy physical grace put me on edge. This was a man who understood his own body and, in turn, understood exactly how to use it to his advantage. Would that grace and his apparent attention to detail prove to be more than I was prepared for? That is, if I actually developed the nerve to seduce the man.

I cleared my throat. "This isn't the sort of relationship I normally allow with artists."

"I'm aware of that."

"I want to tell you no and leave." I looked away from him,

angry with myself for letting him know how uncomfortable I was.

"Then why don't you tell me no and leave?"

I flushed and stared at the platform. "Losing your contract could hurt me professionally."

"And you think I should feel guilty that I've manipulated you into a situation that you find uncomfortable?" He crossed his arms over his chest and stared at me.

"You don't feel guilty?" I raised one eyebrow in question, and wasn't surprised when he looked away from me. "You don't seem the type of man that normally has to resort to such things to gain a woman's time or attention."

"No, most would say that I have an easy time of it with women."

"So, why not just ask me? Did you come to Holman's knowing that you wanted me to model for you?" His expression spoke volumes. Shamus wasn't a man used to having to explain himself.

"I approached Holman's for the show because of you. You were my goal, Mercy. I value the work I've created. So, of course, I want it showcased in the best possible venue, but I could've had any gallery in the city."

"Why didn't you just ask?" I demanded again, more furious than before at his high-handed maneuvering.

"Because you would've told me no."

"So you force me into a position where I can't refuse you." I turned away from him and walked away from the platform. "Don't you think this makes this situation twisted?"

"A little. But I don't let my own discomfort get in the way of what I want."

I believed that. Moving further away from him, I stopped in front of a nearly empty bookshelf that lined one wall. A simple velvet cloth on one shelf held eight miniature women. Each was unique and beautifully crafted. "What are these?"

"They are a project I'm working on for my grandfather."

I glanced toward him briefly and let my gaze go back to the figures as he approached. "They're charming."

"Thank you." He picked up the first piece, carved in rosewood. "This is my grandmother, Lian. She came to the United States with only the clothes on her back, and a child. She had escaped China at a time when it seemed impossible. Once here, she sought out the man who had fathered her child."

"Your grandfather?"

"No. My Aunt Jia is entirely Chinese." He picked up another carving. "This is her. She's a doctor in New York. Once my grandmother realized that she'd never find her lover, she took a job in grocery store in Chinatown. My grandfather met her there, and from all reports, fell in instant lust with her. That lust quickly turned to love. He promised her the world and took in her two-year-old daughter as his own. They've never spent a night apart in their entire marriage.

"Their relationship wasn't an easy one. They had their problems but managed to survive well. They had three sons and a daughter together." He touched the third female figure with a hesitant fingertip. "My mother, Grace, was that daughter. The other women are my uncles' wives."

"No great-grandchildren?"

"All boys." He laughed softly. "Though Grandfather has hopes that one day I will have a daughter. He is one hundred and two, so as you can imagine, he is less than patient about me attempting to meet that demand."

"When do you plan on giving these figures to him?"

"The next time I go to New York." He cleared his throat. "We should begin work."

I moved past him and walked to stand in front of the platform. "I'm not sure I can do this."

"I won't hurt you."

"Men say that every day." I forced myself to remain still as he walked toward me, and stopped just short of touching me.

26

"I'm not like every other man in your life."

"I know that." He wasn't like *anyone* I'd ever met. I took a deep breath. "How long?"

"The first couple of sessions will be around two hours."

Two hours. One hundred and twenty minutes of naked time with a man I didn't know. I took a deep breath and forced myself to look at his face. I wondered if he thought I was crazy. Soap and the slight hint of aftershave teased my senses.

His scent was all male, and something else. After a moment, I placed it. He smelled like sandalwood and Egyptian musk. I wet my bottom lip. Taking my hand, he gently guided me toward the platform and helped me step onto it. His fingers deftly made short work of my safety knot. He spread the robe open and pushed it off my shoulders.

"Trust me."

"What sort of trust would you have me grant to you, a stranger?"

"Trust that I've created beauty all of my life, and never once in all of my thirty-two years have I considered having any part in destroying it." He cleared his throat, his gaze never leaving mine. "My father collected butterflies as a child. When I was eight years old he gave me the collection he'd spent years putting together. I was devastated by all of that lifeless beauty. As you can imagine, my father was at a loss as to how to deal with me."

"Yes. I imagine so." I took in a deep breath when he smiled softly.

"I couldn't understand how anyone could admire beauty and then destroy it in an effort to keep it close. We eventually buried that butterfly collection in a small funeral in the backyard."

"I grew up in an apartment building in New York." I swallowed hard and kept my eyes on his face. I could hardly believe he hadn't glanced down even briefly.

I released my hold on the robe, and a shiver ran down my spine as the silk scraped over my overly sensitized skin and fell away from me completely. I was exposed—vulnerable. Scared that I would please him. Scared that I wouldn't.

Two years had passed since I'd been naked with a man. Being naked for someone was intimate, far more intimate than I'd allowed in a very long time. Somewhere along the way I had granted Shamus the trust he requested.

Exposed and worried, I watched him take a few steps back. I remained still as Shamus's gaze left my face and drifted leisurely over my breasts and then further down. He inhaled sharply, held, and then released the breath as if he'd forgotten how to breathe. His reaction helped me let go of some of the tension I'd had coiling inside. No one can remain unaffected by someone else's admiration.

"Lie down," he said gently.

"On my side?" I asked softly, wishing that my insides would stop shaking.

He nodded silently, held my hand until I was on my knees, and then released me. I met his gaze and saw nothing but approval. God, this man was amazing, and his approval meant more to me than I expected. He backed up a few steps and then stopped to stare. His gaze moved from my toes, up my legs, across my breasts, and then finally to my face.

"Beautiful." He turned and walked across the room and picked up something. He returned to me with a piece of red silk, holding it out in front of him, eyeing it and me. Shamus paused, and then shook his head and walked away once more. He brought back a small pillow this time, which he placed under my head.

His fingers moved through my hair, spreading it out on the small pillow. Then he draped the silk carefully over my breasts. My nipples tightened immediately, stimulated by the glide of soft material. His gentle fingers brushed over my shoulder as the material slid under my arm and fell down behind me. The

silk brushing and falling down my back sent a wave of awareness and arousal down my spine. I looked away from him as
he knelt on the platform in front of me.

Trying to remain motionless as his hands moved over the
line of my hip, I focused on the yet-to-be-touched block of alabaster. Shamus moved his hand to my thigh; he pulled my
left leg forward and slipped the silk between my legs to cover
my pussy. I fought the urge to move toward him, to encourage more intimate touches. Did he want me the way I wanted
him?

The silk, at first cool on my skin, warmed as it brushed
against me. I felt myself flushing, and I tried to think about
something horrible to keep my body from responding to an
attraction he appeared to have no interest in exploring now.
His touch had been so impersonal that I felt bereft. It was difficult to remember that I wasn't in an intimate personal situation. To him, it was work.

I closed my eyes briefly as he brought the silk back over
my thigh, effectively covering my "pink parts," but leaving
me in a state of undress that was unbelievably stimulating.

"I didn't think you covered your models."

He met my gaze and nodded. "It's a shame to cover you.
But when I first saw you, this is what I thought of." He stepped
back from the platform. "Are you comfortable?"

Surprisingly, I was. "Yes."

He left me and returned with a large sketch pad. He sat
down on the floor a few feet from the platform.

"What are you doing?"

"I'm going to spend a few sessions sketching you. Once I
pick the final pose, I'll start working with the stone. The
sketches will allow me to work with the bigger piece when
you aren't here."

I had nothing to do but watch him. And that was enough.

Shamus had powerful, careful hands. Hands that would
glide, and fingers that would move over skin, bringing heat

and pleasure. Would he be a careful lover, or would he lay a woman out beneath him and devour her with his need? I could almost feel his body, strong and graceful, moving against me, between my legs, and then inside me. My womb clenched against nothing, and I bit down on my bottom lip briefly to keep from moaning.

I focused my attention on his face then. It was perfect—the line of his jaw was strong, classic. Angular and masculine in a way that made me want to touch him. He had a great body, defined and muscular without being too much. He was a physical artist, so I expected that.

I'd dated a black man when I was in college, but there was no comparison. The difference was startling. My memories of Brian were a frenzy of physical unions that would make me ache and demand more. Brian had taught me a great deal about myself and how to pleasure a man.

But Shamus was no college boy. Intense and passionate, he was the sort of man most women wouldn't be able to resist, at least on some level. All of his art pieces, even the small ones in his gallery, were sexy and wrought with sensuality. I'd admired his work for years, and now he was sculpting me. If anyone had told me that I'd meet Shamus Montgomery and be modeling for him all in the same day, I would have laughed.

The silence in the room was surprisingly comforting. This was odd because I loved noise and usually had the radio or television playing at home. Why was silence so much easier to endure with him?

"Will you take photographs?"

"No." He looked up and met my eyes. "I never photograph my models."

That was a relief. Having drawings of me was one thing, but full-blown color photos were another matter. What normal woman wanted her ass immortalized in living color?

I cringed at the thought of a camera. It'd come out in therapy that pictures had been taken of me during the rape exam at the hospital. I could still remember the faint click of the camera, and the flash bursting with light. Despite my effort not to react, Shamus had noticed and put down the pad.

"Are you all right?"

"Yes, fine."

Shamus leaned back on his hands and glanced me over. "You seem upset."

"I was just thinking about something unpleasant." I dropped my gaze to the length of floor that stretched out between us. "I'm fine."

Picking up his pad, he went back to work while I tried to push the past away. Lately, it seemed easier to let go of what had happened to me in New York. It was never really far from my thoughts, but now it seemed to hurt less and anger more. It hadn't been easy for me to get past the point of pain and betrayal. Perhaps it would've been easier to get to the angry stage if I hadn't considered Jeff King a friend. Not a close friend, but certainly not a stranger. Until that moment in my office when I realized that he was dangerous, I'd never thought for a moment that he would hurt me.

I glanced toward Shamus and found him working intently. There was something special about him, and it was more than his artistic skill. It amazed me that I could inspire a man like him. He'd traveled all over the world and was one of the most sought-after sculptors in the entire country. His work graced the lobbies of countless buildings around the world. It was no understatement that men and women traveled half the world over to come to the very place I was lying.

He belonged to a world of beauty that I could only look at but never truly be a part of. My passion for the arts, both past and present, sustained me through difficult years with my parents and the move to Boston. Yet I would never truly understand what it's like to be an artist.

I shifted and grimaced as the muscle in my thigh tightened. Sitting still had caused it to cramp up. "I need to stretch."

Shamus stood and walked over to the platform. "Your leg?"

"Thigh." I swallowed hard when he sat down on the platform and motioned me to turn over on my back.

"Let me help."

"Okay." I shifted onto my back and stretched my legs out. That didn't help.

Strong, firm fingers traced the muscle briefly before Shamus used both hands to shift my leg and move it. The red silk fell away from my sex, revealing my pussy and the damp curls that covered it. I watched through half-closed eyes as he gently but firmly massaged my thigh, and sighed when the muscle began to relax under his touch.

"Lift up a little."

I planted my foot flat against the pillow I was lying on and shifted slightly as his hands slid up my thigh, nearly to my hip bone, only to pause and then travel leisurely back down. The man was trying to make me stupid. I bit down on my bottom lip and swallowed hard to keep from making any sounds. He glanced at me then, his gaze drifting over my breasts and then to my face.

"You are a beautiful woman."

"Thank you."

"Is this better?"

I nodded and shifted away from him when he removed his hands. I knew I was fairly close to spreading my legs and begging him to fuck me. "It's fine now."

"I'd like to do a few more drawings."

"Okay."

After a few seconds, he nodded and stood. I watched him regain his place on the floor and pick up his drawing pad. He waited until I'd backed into the position he had arranged and slipped the silk back into place before he started work again. My arousal made remaining still almost impossible.

Suddenly he spoke. "Talk to me."

I frowned. "Talk to you?"

"Tell me about your day."

I sighed. "Well, it was a good morning, but the afternoon was a trial."

"Oh, really?"

"Yep. I was manipulated by an arrogant man into posing naked in his studio."

"Must be really horrible to be so beautiful."

I glanced at him, saw a smile that slipped across his lips as he stared intently at the paper in front of him. "Is that why I'm here?"

"Beauty is a varied and wonderful thing. I've known women who would not fit the traditional definition of beauty but were entirely beautiful to me. Then there are women like you . . . an amazing face and all those curves. My grandfather would say you look like ten miles of bad road. Curvy, challenging, and thrilling to explore."

"And do you want to explore me?"

He lifted his gaze. "In every way possible."

"Do you say that to every woman you bring into your studio?"

He stood and walked over to me. Sitting on the side of the platform, he ran his finger along the line of my jaw.

"Mercy." The gentle way he said my name, combined with the soft drifting of his fingers on my face, made me want to wrap myself around him. "Tell me why you think so little of yourself."

I flushed; not moving was an effort. "I don't know what you mean. I'm lying here, naked. What more could you want?"

Saying nothing, he continued to stare. I felt almost penetrated by his gaze, as if he were reading my soul. His dark eyes took all of me in, and I moved, unable to help myself.

His eyes darkened further, allowing me to see his own response to me. He wanted me, despite the cool exterior he was presenting.

Silent, Shamus watched me fidget on the pillow.

The red silk slid over my skin, and I felt a blush cross my face as my nipples tightened further and pushed against the material. His gaze dropped to my breasts. His tongue darted against his bottom lip. Swallowing hard, I could almost feel his mouth on me. My nipples were so hard they ached. I moved my legs together and watched his gaze move down my body to my legs. I wished that I'd left the silk off. I wanted him to see the damp curls of my sex, so he would know exactly how much I wanted him.

He sighed and stood. "You are wearing more than you think."

"I've done exactly what you've asked of me. What the hell more could you want?" My response came out snappy and hard. I regretted the loss of control, but his pointed dismissal of my sexual response to him had hurt.

"I think you do know what I mean. But you hide from yourself more than you hide from the world."

I watched him walk away from the platform. He turned to look at me as tension stretched between us, then he let his gaze drop to the floor.

He didn't say anything for a long moment, and I found myself unable to let the silence persist. "Why do you care?"

He plucked the robe from the floor. "We're finished."

"It hasn't been two hours." I pressed my lips together briefly. I'd done what he wanted, and his dissatisfaction was infuriating.

"No, but you're too tense for me to continue."

"I'm sorry."

I didn't want to be sorry; briefly, I indulged in a little self-hatred for the apology. The situation was ridiculous. No matter how I tried to justify it, there was no getting comfortable with the idea of posing for him. Telling Shamus Montgomery no seemed impossible. Who was he to come into my life and start to demand my time and attention? I'd considered my life full until he'd presented himself, and resented him for reminding me of the things that had been missing.

"Dress and I'll walk you out."

I stood up and let the silk drop away. He held out a hand to help me step down. I let my fingers curl briefly against his palm before I pulled my hand free. Silently he offered me the robe.

I glanced briefly at the robe, dismissed it, and walked to the dressing screen. I dressed quickly behind the screen, relieved the session was over. Standing there in my sundress, I still felt naked. My clit was throbbing between my labia, and my nipples were still unbearably hard. Clutching my purse, I left the screened area and glared at the reason my body was reacting so strongly.

Shamus stood by the stairs, the door once more open. I lifted my chin and walked to him.

Slipping past him, I went down the stairs. At the bottom, I paused and wondered if the early dismissal meant that he'd changed his mind about my posing. He joined me and walked beside me to the exit.

As he pulled his keys out to let me out, I took a deep breath and said, "Mr. Montgomery—"

"Shame," he corrected. "My friends call me Shame."

I wasn't sure I wanted to be his friend.

"Will you want me to return tomorrow?"

"Yes." He turned the key in the lock and opened the door for me. "We'll order some food in and spend some time together before we try again."

I walked quickly to my car and looked back to him as I pulled open the driver's door. He was standing where I'd left him.

I had no business getting involved with a man, especially

now when my career was on the right track, and I should have been grateful for his restraint. Instead I felt rejected and angry.

I yanked my seat belt into place and turned the car on. He pulled his door shut as my headlights came on. Lust burning in me, I shoved the car into drive and hoped that I would make it home before surrendering to the need to self-pleasure.

I finally inserted my key into my apartment door and shoved it open. The trip home had done nothing to knock the edge off my physical response to Shame. I tossed my keys and purse aside and closed the door with a sigh of relief. Four bolt locks and a chain later, tension started to seep out of my body.

I went into the kitchen and pulled out a bottle of wine. With a generous glass of wine in hand, I moved into my living room. I could still smell him; the musky cologne had followed me home. Drowning in thoughts of Shamus Montgomery, who was plainly stingy with his cock, I took a generous sip of the wine and then set the glass down.

I pulled my dress over my head. My white strapless bra and panties fell on top of the dress. I stood in my sandals for a moment, and then toed them off as I picked up my glass. After a deep swallow of wine, I dipped my index finger into the glass. Wetting my nipples with the liquid, I set the glass aside as my hand slid down my body. I sat down on the couch. The slightly rough material rubbed my skin as my back met with the back of the couch. I covered my pussy with one hand and closed my eyes.

Rubbing the heated flesh I found there, a relieved sigh escaped my lips. I slipped one finger between my labia and flicked my clit carefully. My finger moved back and forth as I thought about the man who had brought me to such a state without even trying. In my mind's eye, I imagined his hands moving over my pale thighs, the darkness of his skin marked against my own. Then his powerful body would move over me, his mouth drawing wet trails down my chest, and his lips pulling at my nipples. My teeth clenched as my orgasm overwhelmed me.

My hand fell from my body. I sought out my wineglass and drained the remaining contents. I hoped Shamus Montgomery was suffering for his self-control as much as I was. It would only be fair. The man had driven me to masturbation twice in one day.

When I could, I rose from the couch and walked into the kitchen to refill my glass. I glanced toward the phone and answering machine.

The message light was blinking madly. I hit the "play" button. The machine hummed, and then all I heard was nothing. A hang-up. I deleted the message and found two more just like it before I got to the final message. The moment Jane started speaking, I smiled.

"You'd better have lots of juicy and nasty things to tell me. My lesbian lover–gay friend thing didn't pan out. I went to the Peach Tree with Susanne, but it freaked me out when women hit on me. Susanne told them that I was her bitch."

"How prisonlike." I glanced toward the machine as Jane continued.

"Yeah, I know what you are thinking. But if I were in prison, I'd definitely want a lover like Susanne." Jane snorted. "Oh, I scuffed my brand-new shoes, and you know how I feel about that."

I did, indeed. Jane worshipped shoes much the same way I did purses. She reminded me of a meeting I had scheduled first thing in the morning, and then was cut off, probably by my machine. Deleting her message, I considered the hangups. It seemed that it was time to change my phone number again.

Uncomfortable with my line of thought, I walked toward the bedroom while sipping my wine. I went to my desk, sat down at my computer. Sitting back in my chair, I watched the e-mail pour into my inbox. There was an e-mail from Martin. I suppose he'd written to see if I'd gotten the wedding invitation. I hadn't e-mailed him or received e-mail from him in more than six months. It had been difficult to contact him after I'd finally realized how much I'd hurt him by leaving New York.

I opened the e-mail reluctantly and sighed. Since there was no way I could go to New York to attend his wedding, I wished that I could simply ignore the e-mail and the invitation. But I couldn't do that: the man had been the center of my world after I'd been raped. He'd taken care of everything, and it was difficult even now to imagine how I could've survived without him. No one had ever understood my pain and horror the way he'd seemed to.

I closed the e-mail message and marked it for reading later. If I ignored it completely, he would call. Then I would have to tell him that I couldn't bring myself to come to New York. In fact, I hadn't gone back since I'd left. My parents had come to me on holidays and birthdays, though they made it clear they found Christmas in Boston less than desirable.

My mother had sent me two chain letters, a joke, and the newsletter for her garden club. I'd never understood why she belonged to a garden club, as she lived in an apartment. Apparently, she thought her window garden counted. I browsed through the newsletter; I knew she wouldn't have sent it if there hadn't been something about her. I found it near the bottom. Julia Witherspoon-Rothell was there, in all of her glory, with a shiny shovel in hand. The article stated that she had broken ground on a community garden in Brooklyn.

Since community gardens had been my mother's passion for more than ten years, it wasn't much of a surprise. But it was nice and somewhat amusing to see her standing there in designer overalls and tidy white athletic shoes. I glanced toward the clock and frowned. It was entirely too late to call her. She went to bed with the sun, and always had. I finished off the wine and went to take another shower.

With lust firmly on the back burner, I was left mildly irritated that I'd responded so strongly to Shame. To be honest with myself, I've never been one to deny myself something. If I wanted it, I usually got it. Being forced to deal with my own needs was a slight blow to my pride, especially needs that had been stoked by a man.

Tomorrow would be a new day, a day that would end with me in front of Shamus Montgomery, naked.

CHAPTER 3

I entered Holman Gallery and tried to ignore the two clerks
on the sales floor who were blatantly staring at me. The
entire damn gallery knew about the deal I'd struck with Shamus
Montgomery. It was difficult deciding whether to be angry or
pleased by that.

Jane was waiting for me outside my office, and the rest of
staff hovered near her desk. Walking past Jane, I took the
coffee she offered and tried to give her a smile as she came
into my office and shut the door firmly behind her.

Keeping that fake smile on my face, I looked Jane right in
the eye. "If you tell a single one of those backstabbing wenches
out there what I'm going to tell you, I'll kill you and destroy
your body in the office shredder."

Jane held up her hand in the universal sign of Scout's
honor, which I've never trusted. "I promise not to tell the
wenches a damn thing. However, I'm going to die if I don't
get some news."

"Fine. I got naked, he sketched me, and then I put on my
clothes and left."

Jane frowned. "That was *not* worth my promise."

"It's a business arrangement." I sat down at my desk and
sighed when my face started to heat. "Business that was so
intimate that by the time it was over I wanted to run for my
life."

"Did he do something weird?"

I glanced up and chuckled at her outraged expression. "Why? Will you go beat him up if he did?"

"I just might."

"No, he didn't do anything weird." I sighed. "He just sat on the floor and sketched."

"Oh." She sat down and glanced briefly out into the bull pen before centering her gaze on me. "Are you going back today?"

"Yes."

"Is your reaction caused just by nerves, or are you genuinely put off by all of this?"

"Well." I sighed and stopped to think before responding. "Okay, it's flattering that an internationally known artist is inspired by me."

"He said you inspired him?"

"Yes."

She blew air between her lips and shook her head. "Wow. Did your ego explode?"

"Well, I couldn't argue against it." Shrugging, I dropped my gaze to the desk in front of me. "He's an amazing and thoughtful man, despite the fact that he tricked me into posing for him."

"I wish a famous, insanely sexy artist would trick me into getting naked."

I laughed as she stood. "Be careful what you wish for."

"Nothing happened?"

"There is something about the man."

"Yeah, there always is something about men who are gorgeous and wealthy."

I laughed and shook my head. "He's arrogant and domineering. I'll admit that I find him attractive. I'd have to be dead not to." I picked up a pen and tapped gently against the glass top of my desk. "I'd really like a solid wood desk."

"It wouldn't match the rest of the office."

I wrinkled my nose. "I don't care."

"What I hate is that I can't take off my shoes at my desk. Anyone that comes near me can see everything." She crossed her arms over her breasts and sighed. "No privacy."

"I think that was Milton's goal." I motioned toward the bull pen. "Look out there, all you see is legs. It's no mistake that ninety percent of the staff is female."

"That's why I wear pants. He's not going to spend his day checking out my legs." She turned in her seat to focus on me. "Nothing happened?"

Her skeptical expression amused me. I suddenly wished that I did have something to share. "Well, I had a cramp in my leg and he rubbed it." I shrugged. "He was a perfect gentlemen."

"That sucks."

"Yeah." I nodded and then glared at her when she smiled. "I didn't say that."

"It's too late to take it back."

"It's business."

"Ah, crap, come on. You were naked with that sexy man, and all he did was draw you. You could at least tell me he drew *on* you. I could live with that." Jane sighed and then crossed her arms over her breasts. "That man is probably the sexiest human being in this city."

Laughing, I shook my head and then sipped my coffee. "It was all perfectly decent."

Jane glanced out towards the bull pen, deflated. "Can I tell Perky Tits that he worshipped you for hours?"

I looked briefly at Sarah and grinned. "You need to stop calling her that. You are going to slip up one day and say it to her face."

Jane stood up and strode toward the door. "How can I live vicariously through you if you have no life?"

She shut the door behind her, leaving me to sit there and digest her words. While it hadn't been her intent, her observation about my lack of a life hurt. I fiddled with a pen, tapped it against my desk, and considered the gaping hole in my personal life. I couldn't very well ignore the fact that I'd had a handful of dates in a year. Two of them had been blind dates, blind dates that had ended so badly I could barely stand to think about them.

I glanced at my phone when it started to ring. I picked it up. "Mercy Rothell."

"It's me."

"Good morning, Milton." I bit down on my lip to keep from groaning aloud. He only called when he wanted to argue with me without having to look me in the eye. Which meant he was going to demand something totally out of the question.

"How did your meeting with Montgomery go?"

"An arrangement was made." There was no way I was going to give that troglodyte the details of how or when I got naked. It was weird enough to think the word *naked* when he was around.

"Good." There was a long pause and then he got to the reason he was calling. "You have an appointment with Lisa Millhouse. You'll be taking Sarah with you. It will be a good experience for her."

"Lisa Millhouse doesn't tolerate strangers." I looked at Sarah's desk and found her staring at me. "Taking your plaything along could potentially ruin the gallery's professional relationship with an up-and-coming artist that the art world is very excited about."

He sputtered and then huffed.

I should learn to keep my opinions to myself. Milton Storey had been trying to get me fired since the Board of the gallery hired me. He hated the shows I arranged, considered Lisa Millhouse's work pornography, and sought out every opportunity to sabotage the gallery's contract with her. Her contract had been my first assignment with the gallery, and getting it signed had gone a long way toward cementing my place at Holman. Our Board had wanted her work for a long time.

"You'll take Sarah," he insisted.

"I will not," I responded gently. "If we were to lose the Millhouse contract and have an empty east wing this summer, the Board would expect it was for a good reason. As far as I'm concerned, entertaining your current piece of eye candy simply doesn't qualify as a good reason."

He hung up on me. That was his usual response when reminded that I was only five months away from taking his job. I shouldn't have rubbed his nose in it, and doing so made me feel malicious and mean. Still, there is something to be said for being mean to someone who drives you insane.

I dried my coffee cup and dropped the paper towel in the trash. The break room was a mess; it always was. It had occurred to me that if the people in the office treated their home like they treated the break room, then I had no interest in being their guest. I sighed and leaned against the counter. Several memos on the subject of cleanliness had gone totally ignored. I had two choices at this point: I could lock the break room, or I could have the cleaning company include the break room in their routine.

It was irritating to think about. I shouldn't have to pay five hundred dollars more a month for a clean break room. I glanced up when the door snapped closed. Sarah stood glaring at me in silence. It seemed that she had finally decided to confront me.

"Sarah."

"I have plans, and you're interfering with them." She crossed her arms over her chest and tightened her jaw as she glared at me.

Well, at least she got to the point. I made sure I did too. "I have plans for this gallery, and they do not include letting an inexperienced buyer deal with clients that are central to those plans."

"Do your plans include fucking the artists you sign to this gallery?"

"No. My career plans don't involve sacrificing my dignity and self-respect." I watched her cheeks flush pink and her eyes harden. "I am your supervisor, and it would serve you well to remember that the next time you decide to have a conversation with me. Holman's is a professional operation, and professional behavior is required."

She turned abruptly and jerked the door open to leave. "Fine."

I watched her leave, mildly irritated. Jane popped her head in then and checked her watch. "Lisa Millhouse is expecting you."

"I know."

"Don't let Perky Tits upset you."

I laughed and snagged my coffee cup off the counter. She handed me the plans for Lisa's show and my briefcase in exchange for the cup. "Thanks."

"No problem." She glanced over her shoulder and shrugged. "You know, if we were in high school, I'd offer to kick her butt in the bathroom."

"If we were in high school, you'd be standing lookout while I kicked her butt in the bathroom." I grinned when she laughed. "Has Mr. Brooks confirmed his attendance this afternoon?"

"Yes."

The drive to Lisa Millhouse's home was relaxing. She lived forty-five minutes outside Boston. Lisa worked in bronze and iron most of the time; there was something very interesting about a woman with a blowtorch. I knew she was starting to experiment with wood and canvas. She'd been creating for nearly eight years, and I was fortunate to have signed her with the gallery.

Lisa was standing on her porch with a cup of coffee in one hand when I pulled into her driveway. The first time I'd met her was over the barrel of a paintball gun. It took me three weeks to gain her trust, and she still regarded me with a bit of apprehension. Since she apparently viewed everyone that way, I didn't hold it against her.

Her work was provocative and sexy in a way that was almost violent. There was nothing quiet about her passion. I took the plans for her new show out of the backseat and waved. With a brief nod in my direction, she went back into the house.

I followed and found her in the kitchen, pouring me a cup of coffee. I took it and placed the plans on her kitchen table. "You look like you haven't been sleeping."

She shrugged and sat down at the table. "The dreams are worse in the summer. I don't know why."

Besides her nasty divorce, I knew very little about her. But I knew all about dreams, at least my own. I wondered if her dreams made her sick with anger and fear. Did she roam her house over, checking windows and doors? Lisa was a mystery in so many ways, and a part of me wanted to drag all of her pain out of her and throw it away. Yet, I knew that some people used pain as fuel. Fuel for passion, rage, and living. What would Lisa be without her pain?

I sat down and pulled the plans from the cardboard tube. "I have the construction crew standing by to start work on the show space. I wanted to make sure you were happy with the arrangement before we began."

She leaned over the plans and studied them carefully. After a few moments, she nodded. "It's good. I like the flow through the space . . ." She paused and then nodded. "I have a piece that is perfect for the center. It'll be the finale for the show."

"Good." I sat back in the chair and frowned into the coffee she'd given me. "You should know that Milton has decided to use you against me."

"Work politics suck." She sat down. "I'm happy with you and Holman Gallery. I'm willing to endure whatever you might have to do in the next few months to secure your job."

"I appreciate that."

"I can't promise that I won't show my ass."

"I know."

"Besides, I find it amusing to thwart a man like Milton Storey." She grinned and chuckled. "I guess I'll need to order some more ammunition for my paint gun."

"God help us." I smiled into my coffee. I wouldn't encourage her, but I wasn't going to tell her what to do either.

"I understand you're posing for Shamus Montgomery."

Crap. I was hoping to avoid talking about him. "Yes, how did you find out?"

"He called me earlier this morning about a shipment of rosewood we purchased together about a week ago. Shame is very good about warning me when delivery men are going to come out here." She glanced my way and laughed. "He's very attractive, don't you think?"

"I suppose so." I shrugged. Shamus was as close to beautiful as a man could get, and she knew it.

"He's also very talented. There are few artists out there that could capture all that you are, Mercy. I can't wait to see what he does."

"His show will open about three weeks after yours and will take up the entire top floor of the north wing." I watched her stand, go to the coffeepot, and refill her cup. "Is there anything I can do?"

"No. I'll get sleep eventually. Do you want to see what I've done for the last project so far?"

I stood and nodded. "Of course."

I followed her out the back door of her house, across a

small, neat lawn, and into the barn she used for her studio. A large bronze sculpture stood in the center of her work space. The feminine lines struck me immediately. It screamed pain and emotional chaos. I glanced at her briefly, disturbed by the honest and hateful emotion that came from it. The female form was in a kneeling position, protecting her head from an invisible threat.

"It's beautiful." It was a cruel beauty.

Desperately wanting to run from it, I closed my eyes briefly. Unwilling but also unable to stop myself, I focused on the sculpture again and swallowed back a hard knot of distress.

"Thank you."

"Lisa, are you sure you want this on public display?"

I met her gaze and found the pain of the sculpture in her eyes. "Yes."

Nodding, I let my eyes drift over the piece one more time. "What will you call it?"

"*Breaking Point.*"

Nodding, I cleared my throat. "You're right. It will be perfect for the finale." I checked my watch, aware that I was seeking to escape. "I've an appointment in about an hour, so I'd better head back."

Lisa chuckled. "One day, Mercy, you'll have to break free of that shell you've created."

I looked toward her. "What do you mean?"

"You love art. Yet you're embarrassed and uncomfortable by the emotion it invokes in you." She inclined her head. "Why do you hide your passion?"

I had no answer to that question. I sighed, let my eyes drift over the sculpture one last time, and then left the barn. She didn't follow, and I didn't expect it. Lisa was one of those people who understood privacy. She valued her own so much that she innately knew when another person felt invaded and needed to be alone.

*   *   *

On the way back to the city, I turned the radio off. Either the noise was too stimulating, or I was oversensitive. It was past lunchtime when I returned to the gallery, leaving me only ten minutes to prepare for the Board meeting that had been scheduled for nearly a month. I hurried through the gallery and up the stairs that led to the administrative area.

Jane was standing at the top of the stairs holding a big chocolate chip cookie, a cup of coffee, and my agenda for the meeting. I took the cookie as she followed me through the bull pen to the large conference room. Two members of the Board were already there. "Remind Mr. Storey of the meeting, Jane."

Jane nodded after she placed my coffee on the table. "Of course."

James Brooks, the chairman of the gallery's Board of Directors, was sitting across the table from me, eyeing my cookie. "I'm not sharing."

He laughed. "You're fortunate that I like stingy women."

That was true. His ex-wife was so tight with money she could make Abe Lincoln spring up from his grave and beg for relief. They'd divorced in a friendly manner more than a year before. I glanced down the table and smiled at her. I'd often wondered how they had managed to stay so damn friendly. I divided the cookie in half and offered it to him with little goodwill. The fiend took it immediately. I munched my half and glanced over the agenda.

"You've read over the final contract with Shamus Montgomery, James?" I asked, hoping that I didn't look too smug.

"Oh, yes. We were pleased with the contract. He rarely offers his work outside his own gallery space."

"He doesn't have much of a choice. His space can't accommodate his new show. Ten of the twenty-two pieces he already has weigh over two hundred pounds." Finishing off the cookie, I picked up my coffee. "Did you hear the rest?"

"Oh, yes." James grinned as the door opened and the three remaining members of the Board entered, followed closely by Milton. "I'm actually looking forward to seeing what he does."

Yeah, I was really looking forward to that myself. I looked down at the table and tried not to think about my boss and various other people I would have to work with seeing me bare asssed and immortalized in alabaster. It *was* a fucking nightmare.

The Board of Directors for Holman Gallery was made of five people: James Brooks, Cecilia Marks, Dr. Natalie Monroe, her husband Carl Monroe, and Victor Ford. I could count on one hand the number of times the last three had spoken. I secretly called them the Silent Trio. Honestly, I was never sure if they were too bored to respond or were communicating telepathically. Maybe they were going to take over the world one day.

I didn't have to wonder long about what Milton was going to say to the Board. The moment he sat down, he started to talk.

"As you know, Ms. Rothell signed Shamus Montgomery yesterday." The members nodded. I sat back in my chair and waited for the rest. "She also agreed to pose for him in the nude. I consider this inappropriate. I also consider Mr. Montgomery's work too raw for the Holman Gallery."

"Shamus Montgomery's last show netted the gallery that hosted him a reported ten million dollars in commissions," I responded. "As for my decision to honor Mr. Montgomery's request that I pose for him . . ." Pausing, I considered my next words carefully. "It is both an honor and privilege to be considered worthy of modeling for his work. I believe the piece will add a special quality to our show and go a long way toward cementing our relationship with the artist. The happier he is with this show, the more likely he will be to return for his next showing."

"The Assistant Director of this gallery has no business strutting around naked for a contracted artist," Milton snapped.

"I don't strut," I returned mildly.

"Mercy has this matter well in hand, and we'll let her deal with it as she sees fit. Now, what about Lisa Millhouse?" James picked up a napkin and brushed cookie crumbs from his sleek, neatly groomed beard.

"She approved the plans for her show in the east wing this morning. I'll start the construction crew immediately. Once we have the space ready, we'll have the work delivered from our storage area. The last piece for her show will have to be retrieved from her studio." I flipped the page in the agenda.

"Good." James glanced briefly around the table and then focused on me. "Now, tell me about your idea."

"I'd like to reopen the south wing of the gallery and hold a series of shows for local high-school students."

"That's ridiculous!" Milton interrupted. He puffed up and glared at me. "Our budget couldn't support a project like that."

Sighing briefly, I glanced toward Milton before returning my gaze to James. "This project would serve several purposes for the gallery. It will bring in potential customers. No parent worth their salt is going to miss seeing their child's work on display in an art gallery. It will strengthen our reputation in the community as a leader and an advocate for youth organizations and the arts in schools."

"The entire south wing?" Milton demanded. "We've had it closed for six months to save money."

"Exactly, it's sitting there empty when it could be serving a valuable function." I bit down on my tongue to keep from going on further.

"I like it."

I looked down the table to Cecilia Marks, the former Mrs. Brooks. She was a patron of the arts and a society maven that could make or break the average woman. She'd made my move to Boston easy. I owed her a lot. Her approval meant a great deal to the Board and me.

"Yes. I like it, too. You can start by contacting the schools to develop a dialogue with the art teachers," James said.

Milton followed me into my office and slammed the door. "In case you missed it, I'm still the director of this gallery."

I rubbed my forehead and sat down in my chair. "The decision has been made, Milton. There is nothing more to discuss."

"I'm going to make you regret coming to Boston, Ms. Rothell."

I already regretted meeting him but didn't suppose that counted. He stormed out of my office.

Jane entered, shutting the door gently. "Well?"

"They said yes."

"Awesome." Jane grinned and sat down in one of the visitor chairs. "I'm so jazzed."

"Once Milton is gone, I'm going to make sure you get full credit for the idea. It chafes that I had to hide it now." The last thing I wanted was to take credit for her idea. The whole thing had been so off-putting that it had taken her several months to talk me into it.

Jane grimaced and then looked out into the bull pen. "If he knew I was involved in it, he would make my life hell. So, thank you."

I nodded and wondered how Jane would feel in August when I recommended her for my position. She deserved it, but I wasn't going to tell her so until the Board approved it. Looking to my watch brought a frown. I only had two hours left before I was once more in Shamus Montgomery's clutches. We sat in silence for a moment, lost in our own thoughts, and then she sighed.

"You should sleep with him."

I jerked and looked at her. "For God's sake."

Jane grinned. "I know you don't believe me, but a well-placed cock has a way of curing what ails you."

"Nothing is ailing me."

"Whatever," Jane muttered and stood up. "I'll let you know if I hear anything about Mr. Storey's plans."

A well-placed cock, indeed. I turned the phrase over in my head and silently agreed. I moved my legs against each other and tried to ignore the empty feeling that centered in my womb. I didn't know why Shamus made me feel empty, but it had also occurred to me that he could fill me beautifully.

The ringing phone jarred me loose from what would have become a filthy daydream. I picked it up and leaned back in my chair as I put the receiver to my ear. "Mercy Rothell."

"Good afternoon, Mercy." His voice was enough to turn my insides to mush.

I leaned back in my chair and turned away from the bull pen. "Mr. Montgomery."

He laughed. "Do you eat Chinese?"

"I do." I twirled my finger around the phone cord and stared out the window.

"Good, that's what's for dinner."

"Why not let me out of this, and find a willing woman?" I bit down on my lip, because suddenly I wasn't all that interested in getting out of posing for him. It was an odd state to be in, both excited and leery.

He was silent for a moment. "It would be a disservice to you to let you back out of posing for me. Aren't you tired of living a half-life?"

I closed my eyes and chewed on my lip. He was baiting me and waiting for me to reveal myself. Finally I responded, "I'll see you at six."

"I'll be waiting."

I ended the phone call and sighed. The fact that a man like Shamus Montgomery would be waiting for me was hard to grasp. He'd come into my life like a force of nature, and I knew that I would never be the same.

"It's not often that you come in like this."

Lesley's tone was even, but I could hear the curiosity in her voice. I must have sounded like a complete psycho when I had called her less than twenty minutes ago and begged to see her.

I shrugged and then shook my head. "There's this man."

"Ah."

Growling with irritation, I pushed the lever on the recliner and crossed my ankles on the footrest. "He's demanding and pushy."

"You like him."

"It would be difficult not to," I admitted, disgruntled. "He's charming, talented, sexy, and—"

"Demanding."

I looked at her and shrugged. "Yeah, demanding."

"Are you afraid of him?"

"No."

"Are you sure?"

"Yes, of course, I'm sure." I frowned at her and then looked away. "I'm sure."

Lesley sighed. "Are you saying that because you want it to be true, or because you think I want to hear it?"

"It's true. The last thing I think about when I look at him is what happened to me in New York."

"What do you think about?"

"Sex. Hard, relentless sex."

"How do you feel about wanting him?"

"It's difficult. I mean, he's hardly the first man that I've been sexually attracted to." I bit down on my lip.

"Is he the first since you were raped?"

"Of course not, there was Martin." I pressed my lips together when I looked toward her. Her disbelief was very obvious. "I was with him for nearly six months before I left New York."

"Yes, you did spend six months hiding in the relationship with your friend Martin."

It sucks when someone you give money to doesn't bother to agree with you even half the time. "Okay, fine, perhaps I wasn't as attracted to Martin as I could've been."

"And your reaction to this new man after two years of celibacy?"

"It takes my breath away," I whispered. "You know, in that romance novel kind of way? I've never felt this way about someone in my life. It's more than wanting him. It's more than anything that I can even define, and I barely know him."

"And you want to know him better?"

"Yes." I frowned and shook my head. "But it's more."

"Just get it out, Mercy."

I sat up and pushed the footrest back into the chair. Nervous, I stood and walked away from the recliner. "There is nothing soft or forgiving about the way I want him."

"Sometimes sex is dirty and violent."

"Yes." I closed my eyes and then took a deep breath. "How can I even think about sex like that after what happened to me?"

Lesley paused and then nodded. "I see." She closed the folder on her desk and folded her hands primly on top of it. "There is nothing wrong with the way you are responding to this man. Sexual desire can manifest in a variety of ways."

"I don't want to be one of those women who needs to feel forced and violated to get off." I turned and looked at her.

"And you aren't."

"Are you sure?"

"Aren't you?" she asked softly. "No one reacts to being violated in the same way, Mercy. You survived it, you've done your level best to put it behind you, and for that you should be proud."

"Okay." I nodded and went back to my chair. "So the fact that I want this man to push me against a wall and fuck my brains out doesn't make me a freak?"

"Think about the types of sex you enjoyed before you were raped. Is it really all that different than what you are wanting with this new man in your life? What was your ideal lover like before you were raped?" She paused and inclined her head. "Did you do the homework I assigned?"

"Not yet."

"Since this isn't a regularly scheduled session, I'll give you a pass for the moment. Just talk to me about sex for the time being."

"I suppose I was like most other women." I shrugged and crossed my arms over my breasts. "Let's see . . . I'm tall for a woman, so I've always found taller men attractive. Strong but careful hands, stamina, and of course a big dick." I laughed softly and shrugged. "I mean, some women will say that it doesn't matter that much."

"But you don't agree?"

"No, I don't. Size matters. It matters a lot. I've always enjoyed men who are comfortable with their own bodies and with a woman's body. I never dug on domination in the extreme, but in the past I liked a man to be strong and in charge. There is something really amazing about giving your pleasure over to someone else. It isn't about giving or taking power."

"It's about trust."

"Yes." I relaxed in the chair a little more. "Okay, so I'm not a freak."

"No," Lesley laughed. "And you wouldn't be much of one if you liked to be to tied down and spanked. There is nothing wrong in domination games as long as the persons involved are of a legal age, find it pleasurable, and no one is damaged permanently."

Damaged permanently. For a moment those words moved around in my head. I'd been forced to realize some time ago that what Jeff had done to me had changed me, and that no matter how much I tried, that he would be with me for the rest of my life. He'd invaded my soul as much as my body, and nothing I could say would change that. Nothing.

The only thing I could do was make room in my life and in my mind for more experiences. If Lesley had taught me anything, it was that my past couldn't be ignored. But more importantly, I couldn't push aside my future forever. I'd channeled all of my energy and ambition into the gallery, and it was beginning to pay off.

With my career goal firmly in sight, my empty personal life seemed to loom larger every day.

"What are you thinking about, Mercy?"

"I don't want Jeff King to dictate how I live the rest of my life, and it seems that I am."

"Explain."

"I don't date men who I'm attracted to because I don't want to risk sexual involvement. I've made all of these plans for my future and my career, and none for my personal life. I haven't let myself think about a husband or even children. Not even five or ten years from now."

"You think this makes you abnormal."

I crossed my arms over my breasts and shook my head. "No. It's just that before I was raped, I could see a man and children in my future. I don't even think about that now."

"You've been in the healing process for a long time, Mercy. Focusing on your career gave you a good way of shaping and controlling your life. You needed that control, and we both know it. Involving a person, another man, takes away some of that control."

"Will I ever be ready for it?"

"Of course."

I laughed softly. "You say that like it's a given. But I've heard about women who never recover from it. They end up locked in their apartments, afraid to leave, afraid to trust even themselves."

"You're on a good path, Mercy."

I nodded. "Okay."

I exited my therapist's office building and pulled out my cell phone. It had vibrated twice while I'd been in the session. Both numbers had been unknown. I was wondering why I paid for caller ID when it started to ring again. It was an unknown number again. Frowning, I pushed "on" to connect the call.

"Hello."

"How are you, Mercy?"

I closed my eyes and opened my car door with a shaking hand. Secure behind the locked car doors, I forced myself to respond. "Jeff."

"I've been thinking about you."

"Funny, I pay someone a great deal of money to help me forget you exist," I responded and was, for the moment, proud that I wasn't in tears. "How did you get this number?"

"That'll be my secret for now. I'd like to see you."

"No."

"We are civilized and educated adults. Meet with me."

Hearing his voice was painful, almost in a physical sense. I could remember the bite of his fingers on my arm, hard words that had told me plainly that he would hurt me more if I fought. But more than that physical reminder, there was the betrayal of our friendship and my trust. Before it had happened, I would have considered Jeff King a friend. Now he was a living, breathing nightmare, and every time he broke into my life I was reminded exactly how foolish I had been.

"The answer is no, and it will remain no." My words

came out strong and convincing. At least my voice wasn't betraying how I felt on the inside.

Carefully, I ended the call and turned off my cell phone. It was as if the whole world was out to make every waking moment of my day as difficult as possible. Embarrassed that I'd suddenly developed a persecution complex, I started my car and pulled into traffic.

CHAPTER 4

Once more, I found myself sitting in front of Shame's brownstone. The drive over had done little to calm me. Jeff's voice was still moving around in my head, and I could almost smell his aftershave. I rubbed my face, undeterred by the damage my damp palms did to my makeup.

Since cowardice was not an option, I got out of my car and set the alarm. Bravery just plain sucks sometimes. Squaring my shoulders and gearing myself up for the pleasure of Shame's company, I entered his gallery. The showroom lights were already down, and the PRIVACY sign was gone from the stairs.

The silence in the room was wretched, and made my stomach tighten. Though I hated to admit it, the conversation I'd just had with Jeff King had set me on edge. His ability to wrench me from the secure world I'd built around myself was overwhelming. But I could only blame myself. If I'd pressed charges, he might've gone to jail.

Looking toward the stairs, I wondered where Shame was. It was the first time he hadn't greeted me in the gallery. I pushed the door to set the bells off again and then moved further in. "Should I lock up?" I called out.

My question fell on the silence of the gallery. Then a decidedly female form appeared at the top of the stairs and stomped down them. Shame was fast on the woman's heels.

She glared at me as she buttoned her blouse. She had a

sleek figure, and for all of her anger, looked like an angel. It was easy to see how an artist could find her inspiring. I understood the look on her face. Women like her weren't familiar with rejection. The same look of shock and confusion must have been on my face the night before. Even now, anger surfaced at the way Shame had ignored my obviously heated body and forced me to deal with my own pleasure.

"Her? You replaced me with her? You ungrateful bastard." The woman glared at him and then ran out the door.

I jumped a little as the string of bells clanged against the glass. Going back to the door, I locked it and pulled the key out. Carefully, I closed the blinds and turned to look at him. "She didn't look pleased."

He shook his head and sighed. "She's young."

"Yes." I walked toward him and offered him the key. "Am I her replacement?"

"No. I used her in two earlier pieces in the collection. She wasn't a fit for the last piece, and disagreed with me on the matter." He pulled the key from my fingers and dropped it into his pocket.

I wanted to ask if she was his lover, but didn't. Meeting his gaze, I realized he was staring at me. "I'm ready."

"No, you're not, but you will be. I had the food delivered."

He took a step back from the stairs, allowing me to go up ahead of him. The platform was gone, and in its place was a large red chair. I stared at it for a moment and wondered what Shame was up to. What made a man like Shamus Montgomery tick? What were his hang-ups? Did he hate mornings like I did? I focused on him then and cleared my throat.

"Maybe we should just get to work."

He motioned toward a table and two chairs. "I think we should eat first."

Glancing briefly at the table, I returned my gaze back to the large red chair. "Restroom?"

He motioned toward a door near the stairs that led to the third floor. "Take your time."

I glanced at him briefly before hanging my purse on a chair and going into the small restroom. One glance in the mirror told me why he'd suggested I take my time. What was left of my makeup only served to highlight my pale features.

It occurred to me that I was in no condition on an emotional level to deal with Shamus. The night before had been difficult, but I felt like I'd held my own. Tonight was different. My emotions were raw, and I felt tainted because of my conversation with Jeff. Suddenly, I just didn't think that all the time I spent in Lesley's office had done a whole lot for me. Shouldn't I be past this phase? Why did that son of a bitch's voice still make me shake?

I washed my face with the hand soap on the sink, grimacing at the knowledge that it would dry my face out. I took a peek in the small medicine cabinet and found a small bottle of moisturizer. It wasn't what I would've chosen, but it would have to do.

Realizing that I'd spent nearly ten minutes in the bathroom, I forced myself to open the door and walk out. Shame was on the opposite side of the room I'd left him in, standing in front of the chair.

I sat down, grabbed a carton of kung pao chicken, and resolved to meet the coming torture with a full stomach. From my position at the table, I watched him walk across the room and join me. My gaze went back to the chair several times before I settled on his face.

"The chair makes you worry?"

Make me worry? The damn thing had my insides tumbling around. Was that what he'd intended with it? The chair was bold, big beyond anyone's needs. I felt like it might swallow me. "Isn't that the purpose of it?"

"It occurred to me that you might like some defined space."

"Space?"

"Yes, space. Space that won't be intruded upon. Whether you believe it or not, Mercy. it is not my intention to make you so uncomfortable that you get sick over it."

"I'm not afraid of you."

"No, I don't imagine you're afraid of much."

Brushing my hair back from my shoulder, I met his gaze. "I try not to be."

"What are you afraid of?"

"I'm no different than anyone else in this world. I suppose the loss of control is my biggest fear. Aren't most fears rooted in that?"

"I would say so, yes." He looked down at his food briefly and then leaned back in his chair to look at me.

I asked him, "What do *you* fear?"

"It's an odd thing, thinking about what I'm afraid of. When I was a younger man, I suppose most of my personal fears involved rejection of my work or maybe myself on a personal level. I've never liked being told no, not even as a child. These days I have very little reason to fear rejection on either level. As an artist, I've carved a niche for myself that is comfortable but not so comfortable that I don't get a bit nervous when I take a risk."

"And on a personal level?"

"I've known enough women to know that for every one that will say no, there are several others who will say yes." He drank deeply from a bottle of water. "My parents gifted me in the genetics department, and I take care of myself. The rest will either come or it won't."

"And when a woman rejects you?"

He grinned. "It's her loss."

"No anger?"

"No. I am entirely too old to get caught up in that game. A woman is either available to me or she's not."

"Yet you tricked me into posing for you."

"That's different. The steps I'm willing to take on a professional level are entirely different than the ones I'd take on a personal level. The fact is, if my interest in you had been merely personal, I would've approached the situation much differently."

He pushed his untouched food aside, and I wondered briefly why he didn't seem interested in eating. Did *I* make *him* nervous? It was a tantalizing if rather impossible notion. "So, you aren't interested in me on a personal level."

"I didn't say that." He smiled briefly, and I felt like punching him right in the mouth. "You know you're beautiful."

"I've been told that before." Picking up a fork, I speared a piece of chicken. "When I was younger I found the attention of men very discomfiting. Not that I ever wished I were ugly, I just often found myself frustrated because people never tried to see beyond my face."

"And what is beyond that charmingly beautiful face?"

"I have degrees in business and art history. If all goes well, I'll be the director of the Holman Gallery in August of this year. I'm an only child, born to a set of disappointed parents who didn't imagine that their daughter would turn out so different from them." I opened the bottle of water he'd set out for me and took a deep drink.

"Are your parents truly disappointed in you, or is that something you imagine to be so?"

Laughing, I couldn't help but shrug. "Well, it's obvious I'm not what either of them imagined I would be. If they'd realized I would never share their insane need for social standing, they might have had another child. They don't understand why I choose to work, how I can possibly function outside of New York, and why I don't settle down with some narrow-minded little man from the social set and give them a grand-child."

"Is there a man in your life?"

I dropped my gaze to my food. "No."

"Tell me why you choose to be alone."

"Just because you've backed me into a corner, Mr. Montgomery, doesn't mean I'm going to bare my soul to you."

"Do you want to know what I see, Mercy?"

"No." I looked at him. "But I have a feeling you're going to tell me anyway."

He laughed and leaned his chin on his hand as he looked over my face. "I see a woman who works too hard at looking happy instead of being happy. The first time I saw you, you struck me as a woman who had control of her world. That was more than two years ago when you worked in New York. What happened there that changed you?"

"I don't remember ever meeting or seeing you in New York." Surely that was something that I would've remembered.

"No, we never met. Though we have a mutual friend in Edward Morrison." He paused briefly. "Why did you leave New York?"

"I found that museum work wasn't my passion. Discovering an artist is far more exciting than protecting the work of those long dead. Life is about living. Museums are about the past." I'd said that same thing more than twenty times since I'd come to Boston, and I still didn't sound convincing. But since I couldn't fathom telling anyone that I'd run from New York because I was afraid of Jeff King, it was all I had to work with.

"There is more."

I met his gaze. "You're pushing me, Mr. Montgomery. I don't like it."

He leaned back in his chair. "I'd assumed that you weren't a natural redhead."

His blunt reminder of how intimate our situation had been the night before was like cold water on my skin. Pushing my plate to the side, I stood. "I'm finished."

He stood, walked to the red chair, and looked toward me. "Then come here."

Walking toward him, I gave myself a mental shake. It was imperative that I not let him rattle me. "I'll just go get into the robe."

"No." He looked me over. "Here. Take off your clothes right here."

Glaring at him, I stopped. "What game are you playing with me, Mr. Montgomery?"

"I told you to call me Shame."

"As if I'd take orders from you." I resisted the urge to cross my arms over my breasts. The need to control the situation was overwhelming, and I knew that Jeff's call was partly responsible. "I'm not a stripper."

He laughed then and took a step back from the chair. "No, you're not." He sat down on the floor a few feet from the chair, sketch pad in hand.

"I would prefer to undress behind the screen."

"Do you always get your way?"

Pursing my lips, I stood and glared at him for a moment. "Does that make you think I'm spoiled?"

"No, you are by far the least spoiled woman I know." He tilted his head briefly. "I thought we agreed last night that you could trust me."

"You asked me to trust you."

"And your trust is not so easily given," he murmured in response. "Undress for me, Mercy."

I walked to stand in front of the chair and pulled my blouse from my skirt. With shaking fingers, I started to un-button it. By the time the last of the buttons were undone, my hands were still. Refusing to look at him, I shrugged the blouse off and dropped it on the floor in front of him.

Our eyes met as I started to unfasten the front clasp of my bra. The room was too quiet. I swallowed hard and let the clasp go, and my bra fell from my hands to the floor. My fingers were nearly numb when I pulled at the tie of the wrap-around skirt I was wearing. Finally, I stood before him in thigh-high stockings, panties, and a pair of flimsy strappy sandals.

"Leave the rest on."

I looked at the chair and dropped my hands to my sides. "The chair is my space."

"Yes." His eyes drifted over me, taking in the hard points of my breasts and then moving downward to the sandals. "And I won't invade that space unless you ask."

"And if I never ask?"

He laughed. "I think we both know that you will. For now, let's concentrate on the work."

"Okay." I sat down and he stood up, putting his pad and charcoal on the floor.

"Sit back in the chair and spread your legs."

Flushing, I did as he requested. "Where do you want my hands?"

"On the arms of the chair." He circled the chair, twice nodding, and then stopped in front of me and stared. "I don't understand you, Mercy."

"There's not much to understand."

"There is." He stepped back from me. "Lean back in the chair."

I sucked in a breath, did as he directed, and tried to ignore the way my nipples were starting to tingle. He went back to his sketch pad, seemingly satisfied with my position.

He said nothing for thirty minutes. He filled three sheets of paper with different perspectives of me in the chair, focusing on my legs. The sketches were spread out on the floor in between us as if he were making a puzzle of sorts. Then he moved to my upper body and face. I shifted a little restlessly but tried to keep the pose he'd arranged. When his eyes settled on mine, he sighed and shook his head.

"What?"

He set down the pad. "Your eyes betray you, Mercy."

"What are you saying?"

"You're a beautiful woman, you brim with sensuality, and yet I see a reserve in you that is misplaced. Women made like you aren't meant to be reserved little kittens. Demure blushes are for the untried. A girl hides away, denies her sexuality. A woman embraces it and her own pleasure."

"You think you see a lot."

"I do see a lot." He inclined his head. "You wanted me last night. Your body was flush with it." His gaze traveled over my nipples, and they seemed to tighten further under his scrutiny. "Yet you made no attempt to encourage an advance. A woman makes her needs clear."

I glared at him, disgruntled that he saw so much. "I will not fall at any man's feet and beg for cock. I can buy one if I want one so badly."

He laughed and nodded. "Yes, I suppose you can. There is no need to open yourself up to rejection or admit your needs when you've got a mechanical device at home at your beck and call."

I crossed my arms over my chest and resisted the urge to flip him off. The arrogant bastard was working on being punched in the face. As if he knew it, I heard him sigh, and turned to look at him.

"Stand up and stretch." He leaned back on his arms and looked me over. "And then remove the rest of your clothing."

I did as he ordered. The control he had over the situation only added to my ire. We both knew that I had no way out of our agreement, and while he appeared to have some remorse about his methods, he had no intention of releasing me from the deal I had unwittingly made. I took my panties off and then sat down to remove my thigh-highs.

Naked once more, I thought. The flimsy shield of my panties that had protected the delicate flesh of my pussy was gone. Arousal sprung forward immediately. Being naked with this man had a way of making my physical world burn. A gentle wetness rushed against my clit, and I swallowed hard, ignoring the urge to put my hand over my pussy and hide.

Shaking a little, I looked toward him. "The same position?"

"No." Inclining his head, he looked over my face. "Get comfortable, Mercy."

I sat back fully in the chair and pulled my legs up against my chest. Wrapping my arms around my legs, I rested my chin on my knees. When I finally looked in his direction, he'd returned to his drawing, seemingly pleased with the position.

After about forty minutes, he closed the drawing pad and stood. "You can dress."

I picked up my clothes as he walked away. Without looking to see where he was going, I hurried to the dressing screen. When I came out from behind the screen, he was sitting in the chair, a glass of wine dangling in one hand. The image was casually elegant and unpracticed.

"I thought that was my space."

He glanced me over casually before meeting my gaze. "Only when you're naked."

"Are you getting what you need?"

He nodded. "Yes, exactly what I need. What do you need, Mercy?"

"What does any woman need?"

"I don't care what any woman needs. I want to know what *you* need."

"Peace," I whispered. "All I've ever needed is peace, Shame."

"Peace is no easy thing to provide." He was silent for a moment and then he nodded. "And it is a difficult thing to gain on one's own."

I walked across the room and picked up my purse. Pulling out my keys, I shoved the thigh-highs and my panties into the bag and zipped it. He stood and followed me as I went to the door and down the stairs. At the front door, he pulled the key from his pocket and then paused.

"I've spent most of my adulthood in the company of beautiful and naked women. Women come to Boston just to pose for me." He met my gaze and cleared his throat. "I've always had a rule about my models."

"Oh, really?"

"Yes." He nodded, gripping the key tightly in his hand. "I don't sleep with them."

"Not even the one from earlier?"

He laughed and shook his head. "No, not even her. Though she did make herself available."

"Have you ever been tempted?"

"Yes." He moved closer. "In fact, I find myself in a dilemma at the moment."

"I tempt you?"

"Yes, but I'm trying to maintain a professional distance until the project is finished."

"I see." I looked down at my shoes and then looked up to his face. "That sounds like a good plan, Shame."

"Yes." He nodded in agreement.

He said something sharp under his breath and then slipped his fingers into my hair to cup the back of my head. He pulled me toward him and covered my mouth with his. I fell into the kiss without hesitating. It was so easy to sink into his mouth and his taste. Two years without the intimate touch of another human being had affected me in ways I'd never noticed. His tongue brushed against my lips and into my mouth. I accepted the invasion for what it was and hoped like hell he wouldn't stop.

Shaking, I clung to him as he pressed me against the door. The blinds clinked against the glass and dug into my back as he ground his body against mine. Held so close to him, I could feel the emptiness build deep down inside. I curled my fingers into his shoulders and pulled my mouth from his with what little self-control I had left. We stayed still, heat pressed against heat, breathing heavily.

"I could smell your need clinging to the chair." His mouth moved along my jaw. "Just thinking about it could make me come."

I tightened my fingers in the fabric of his shirt. "Kiss me."

He took my mouth without further encouragement. I started whimpering as I moved one leg against his. When the need to start begging emerged, I pulled my mouth from his and looked away from him. His hands slid down over my hips, and he took a shuddering breath.

"You aren't wearing any panties, Mercy."

"Yeah." I took a deep breath. "I feel rather naughty about it."

"You should." Shame brushed his lips across mine, and I moaned a little when he deepened the kiss briefly, then lifted his head. "You know I think you're beautiful."

"It's nice to hear it." He moved closer and pressed the hard ridge of his cock firmly against my hip. I didn't need the reminder, but I reveled in it. "And feel it."

"This is too soon." His lips moved across my jaw to my neck.

"Then we should probably stop." I moved, and the shades clinked against the glass.

"In a minute." Shame slid his hand into my skirt, parting it where the material overlapped.

I gasped and closed my eyes as his hand cupped my sex. One blunt finger slipped up between my labia and teased at my clit. "Oh God."

He moved his finger then, and dipped into my entrance. My grip tightened on him as I accepted the sweet invasion of his fingers. The shallow penetration made me weak all over, and I tightened my grip on his shoulders.

"Are you wet for me?"

The question made my insides clench up. I'd been wet for him since I'd set eyes on him. "Shame."

"I know." He pulled his hand away, and I shuddered at the abandonment. "Easy."

"I need more." The admission felt weak, and I closed my eyes.

"Do you need me, or will any man do?"

The whispered question was like a slap in the face. I jerked free of his hold and crossed my arms over my aching breasts. "That's a fucked-up thing to ask."

"I've a right to know if your attraction to me is casual."

I was insulted, but inwardly I agreed that he did have a right to know. The fact was, I wanted him in a way that was alien to me. "I doubt any woman has ever considered a sexual relationship with you casual." I glanced at him briefly. "I don't have meaningless sex. I'm old enough to know better."

He unlocked the door and looked at me. "Good night, Mercy."

"Good night." I wanted to touch him, but didn't. Slipping past him, I walked through the door and out into the night.

Once in the car with the doors locked and my keys in the ignition, it took me several minutes to gather my wits enough to start my car. I could still feel his lips on mine, his tongue slipping into my mouth, his hands moving over me, and finally those fingers dipping into me. I both anticipated and dreaded our next meeting.

I turned on my cell phone and quickly dialed Jane's number as I put my car in drive. The cord to the earpiece tangled in my hair briefly, but I got it straightened out before she picked up. I spoke as soon as I heard her voice. "Give me four good reasons to have wild, up-against-the-wall jungle sex with a man you barely know."

"Orgasm, orgasm, orgasm, and if you don't give him your real name he can't hassle you later."

Laughing, I shook my head. "Thanks."

"No problem. I am the single voice of reason for the modern upwardly mobile woman." She popped her gum before continuing. "So, did you jump his bones?"

"Nope."

"That sucks," Jane sighed.

"Yeah, it's beginning to." With a frown, I stopped at a light. "Say, did you call me and hang up on my answering machine?"

"Nope, I usually hang up before the damn thing answers. You know those things piss me off."

"We all have our mechanical axes to grind. Did you want to meet for breakfast?"

"Let's see . . . Do I want to get up at the ass-crack of dawn to have breakfast with a woman who didn't get laid tonight?" She paused for effect. "No. Hit me back with that offer when you have something juicy to share."

I glanced back at the door of the gallery as I tossed my cell phone in the passenger seat of my car. I wish I had something juicy to share. I could've pretended that I didn't know why he'd sent me on my way, but I knew. Shame wasn't the sort of man who liked women to be coy. If I wanted to be in his life I would have to make my needs very clear to him.

I pressed my thighs together and tried to ignore how my clit still throbbed. The man had me twisted up in a pleasant if frustrating way. Remembering the feel of his fingers slipping into my pussy, I knew it was only a matter of time before my body started making the decisions for me. How much more could I take?

CHAPTER 5

Around 8:30 A.M., I seriously began to regret not having breakfast. I blamed Jane—it was unfair, but it worked for me. I could hear the faint buzz of saws coming from the east wing of the gallery, where Lisa's show space was being prepped. Glancing out into the bull pen, I tried to remember exactly why I'd thought the woman sitting in the chair across from me was worth bringing in from Chicago. It wasn't my money, but I hated the waste. I also hated interviews. This was certainly a task I would be passing along to someone else once I was Director.

"So, Ms. Banks, tell me, what can you see in Holman's future?" I asked.

"Holman Gallery is certainly on the fast track. The contract with Shamus Montgomery you mentioned makes certain that the gallery will not lack for controversy. Controversy sells art. However, it doesn't always give a gallery staying power."

"Please continue." I felt confident that she was going to tell me I was going to hell for encouraging pornography.

"I can bring clients to Holman who will appeal to populations not interested in sexualized art. You mentioned the gallery is going to start an outreach program for high schools? You'll want areas of the gallery that you can guide the parents of these young people to. Art doesn't always have to be violent or provoking."

"I think art must always provoke. If it provokes nothing, then the creator obviously didn't do his job. Art should make you cry, ache, and dream. If it doesn't, then it's a waste of space." I sat back and let her chew on that.

"It appears that you have very specific plans for Holman's."

"I've created a vision for the future of Holman Gallery I promised to deliver, and I will." Standing, I offered her my hand. "Ms. Banks, Jane has your travel arrangements made. I hope your flight back to Chicago is a pleasant one."

The woman beat a hasty retreat from my office, and I walked toward the window. I heard Jane enter and shut the door. When I turned, she was slumped in the chair the formidable Ms. Banks had abandoned. I spoke. "She thinks I'm the female Larry Flynt."

Jane shrugged. "She's one of *those* people. You know, when I was younger my mother would shout out across the yard, 'Jane Cornelia Tilwell, will you stop running around like a heathen! What will people think?'"

"I always wondered who *they* were. Cornelia?"

"Shut up." Jane looked at her shoes and sighed. "I bought some new shoes yesterday while you were at Montgomery's *not* getting laid."

Fingering my diamond pendent, I glanced at her briefly before focusing on the parking lot. "He kissed me."

"Really?"

I laughed. "Yeah."

"And?"

"And my insides melted. I've been attracted to men before, Jane, but he's different. I can't even explain it. Thank God I won't have to see him tonight."

Jane snorted. "You're going to keep your date with the Nerd of the Month?"

"I am a woman of my word, and Jerry is not a nerd."

"He's so much a nerd that regular nerds wouldn't hang out with him." Jane grinned then and would've laughed if I hadn't glared of her.

"How do you know?"

"Because that's the kind of man you date. Boring, nerdy, tidy, men with stock portfolios and absolutely no sex appeal."

"You don't date men unless they have, at least, an undergraduate degree."

"Yeah, but the men I date also have to be fuckable."

"Fuckable?"

"Yes, fuckable. I wouldn't even think about going out with a man if I couldn't imagine myself fucking him."

"I don't engage in casual sex."

She grinned. "There is nothing casual about it if you do it right."

I thought briefly about Shame's question the night before and sighed. Since thinking about him would make for a very unproductive day, I pushed those thoughts aside and put my mind to a problem I thought I could deal with.

"Send Sarah in, will you?"

"Will you turn on the intercom so I can listen?" She arched one eyebrow.

"No."

Jane sighed. "I'm in dire need of real entertainment. Maybe the sexy delivery guy will bring a package today." She strolled out of my office with a little wave over her shoulder.

This was not a conversation I wanted to have, but it had occurred to me that Sarah needed to know that she was being used. Since our conversation in the break room, I'd thought about how I was going to handle her. When Sarah arrived, she shut the door quietly and walked toward me, then chose a chair in the middle of the grouping.

"Sarah, I realize that you view me as an obstacle."

"More like a temporary detour."

Snippy little bitch.

I smiled and rested back fully in my chair. "I will be the Director of this gallery come August. Your future after that will be up to you and your ability to work. It won't matter what Milton has told you or what he's promised you."

"You aren't the Director yet."

"Milton Storey is using you, Sarah. You and I both know it. He's making every effort to push you into situations that will affect my ability to adhere to the Board's wishes."

"He's a powerful man."

"Of course he is. No man with the kind of money he has could be anything else in Boston. What you've failed to realize is that you mean nothing to him. The man married his money, and he isn't going to leave his wife for you. When he retires in August, he'll be in no position to further your career at Holman."

I watched her as she lowered shaking hands into her lap. "You don't know what you're talking about."

"You aren't the first woman he's used this way."

"I'm not stupid, no matter what you or Ms. Tilwell might think. I am very capable of doing my job."

"You wouldn't be here if I thought otherwise. Do you honestly think Milton protected you during that time? I have the authority to hire and fire directly from the Board."

"I can take care of myself, and I don't need or want your advice."

"Ambition is a double-edged sword." I spread my hands out on the blotter, palms flat, and took a deep breath. "And women who sleep their way to power do nothing to further the cause of equality and success for honest, hardworking women."

She stood abruptly. "Are we done?"

"Yes."

She stomped out and shut my door with a loud thump; there was yet another person in the office out to break my measly glass wall. Jane hopped right up and shot toward the lounge where Sarah had disappeared to. I was sure to get an earful later.

Two hostile confrontations in two days wasn't exactly what I'd hoped for, but it only confirmed the thought that Sarah would have to be replaced after Milton was gone. I couldn't afford to have anyone like her on staff. Though I sort of considered her a challenge, I had no room for challenges in the plans I had for Holman after August.

I rubbed my face and considered the conversation I'd been putting off since I'd reviewed my calendar. While I didn't expect Shame to be confrontational about my having to skip a session with him, I did expect to have to make up for it. I wondered what sort of deal he'd wrangle out of me.

Picking up my phone, I dialed Shame's number and started trying to figure out how to tell him that I had a date tonight and couldn't sit around naked for him. He picked it up on the third ring. I said, "Hey, are you busy?"

"Not for you."

I grimaced, his voice was so sexy and nice. It was going to totally suck if he didn't react the way I expected. "I have a date tonight. One I made prior to my agreement to pose for you."

"I see." His tone had cooled considerably, which was irritating. Did the man think that I'd had no life before he walked into it?

"Canceling at this hour would be rude."

"And if I were the man with the date I would be pissed."

"You're the man with the appointment."

"Indeed, the man with the appointment." He sighed. "It's all good. But to make it up to me, you'll have to come over first thing in the morning."

"I usually clean my apartment on Saturdays." Okay, a lie. A big, fat lie. I normally slept in on Saturdays and spent my day in my panties.

"Sacrifice the date or the dusting; it's your choice, Mercy."

"Fine. What time?" I pressed my lips together and frowned.

"How about eight?"

"Yeah." Eight in the morning on a Saturday was meant for sleeping, and anyone who thought differently was crazy.

Disgruntled, I ended the call and looked at my calendar again. It hadn't changed. The date wasn't an exciting prospect, and I resented that. To be honest with myself, it hadn't been exciting before Shamus Montgomery, either. I looked up at the door to my office as it swung open. Damn, that squeaky noise was annoying. Milton strolled in and sat down.

"Sarah will be completing the details on Lisa Millhouse's show."

I raised an eyebrow and then grinned. "Sounds interesting."

He jumped a little, I guess surprised that I hadn't exploded. "Do you have everything she'll need?"

I pulled Lisa's file free from my to-do stack and tossed it on the corner of the desk. "That should be everything."

He snatched the folder and walked briskly out of my office. I watched him take the folder to Sarah. I wondered when the guilt would kick in. Nope, it wasn't coming. I motioned Jane in and pursed my lips; it really wasn't going to come. No guilt. Jane shut the door, and I shrugged.

"I'm going to hell," I announced.

"What did you do?" Jane asked softly.

"Milton just gave Lisa's show to Sarah, and I didn't voice one single complaint." Lisa was going to tear Sarah to shreds.

Jane's mouth dropped open, and then she giggled. "Oh, that's so damn evil."

I watched Sarah Johnson walk stiffly to her desk. She'd been gone less than two hours. That was probably a record for Lisa. Sarah's normally perfect hair was a little bit out of place, and several bright red splotches adorned her white linen suit. I glanced at Jane sitting at her desk and then turned in my chair so they wouldn't all see me laughing like a loon. When I had myself contained, I turned back around and looked toward Sarah's desk. Milton was standing there, listening to what I'm sure was a fantastically funny story. I was almost jealous. He looked furious.

He looked toward my office and hurried across the bull pen. I sincerely wished my wall wasn't glass at times like this. He threw open the door and then slammed it shut. "Lisa Millhouse shot Sarah with a paint gun."

"Yes, I noticed Lisa has changed colors. The first six times I went to see Lisa I got blue. On the seventh try, I'd managed to find a dress the same color as her paint. She was so amused she let me come in." Inclining my head, I met his gaze. "I told you, Milton, that Lisa Millhouse is intolerant of strangers. You chose to ignore my advice, and you sent an inexperienced buyer out to harass an established client. You can be certain the Board will be informed of this."

"You mentioned none of this this morning."

"Frankly, I am tired of repeating myself." I leaned back in my chair. "I've told you repeatedly that Sarah is not ready to operate on her own with artists. Beyond that, you've ignored my opinion on the matter of the Millhouse account for weeks. If your recent act has damaged that account, you can be assured that the Board will know about it."

"The damn woman is ridiculous!" he shouted and then glared at me as if it were really my fault.

"Lisa Millhouse does not ask much of anyone. She expects privacy, and she gets it. I know that Sarah was given several verbal warnings before Lisa took aim because that's what happened with me. Lisa is a talented and passionate artist that Holman is honored to represent."

He glared at me and then left. Sarah was at her desk, being

comforted by one of her friends, and Jane was bouncing in her seat. As soon as Milton was gone, she jumped up and hurried into my office. She shut the door and leaned against it. "I'm about to burst."

"I know. That used to be a lovely suit."

Jane bit down on her lip. "You're killing me. Want to take an early lunch?"

I pulled my purse from my desk and stood. "Yeah, let's go find something bad for us."

"The waiter has a nice ass."

I glimpsed from my menu to the ass in question and then back to Jane. "Yes, he does."

Jane closed her menu and watched the waiter while I considered my choices. The same waiter came around and took our orders. Once that was finished, I looked at Jane. I knew she had something on her mind, and wondered what it was.

"Go ahead."

Jane flushed and started mutilating the cover to her straw. "Can this be a friend-to-friend discussion instead of a boss-to-assistant discussion?"

"Yes, of course. Is something wrong?"

"No." Jane shook her head quickly and dropped the disgraced paper in front of her. She looked at it for a moment. "I want your job when you're promoted in August. I think I deserve it more than anyone else at Holman's."

For a minute, I was silent. It had been my hope that she would be afraid to bring the matter up, which I suppose makes me a horrible person. I couldn't stand the thought of her being disappointed if it didn't go through. "I agree and plan to propose that very thing to the Board in August."

Jane released her breath. "Why didn't you tell me?"

"Because I didn't want you to be disappointed if the Board disagreed with me." I looked up and met her eye. She shook her head and smiled. "I'm serious."

"I know." Jane sighed. "That's so sweet, Mercy."

I rolled my eyes and swished my straw around in my glass. "Too bad you messed it up." I grinned and glanced around the café we'd chosen for lunch. "You know, those paint pellets hurt when they hit. I can't believe she took three before she ran."

Jane laughed. "I heard her say that if you could win Lisa Millhouse over, she knew she could."

"Perhaps if Lisa liked women," I responded dryly and then leaned back in my chair. "Milton thinks with his dick. It's just too bad that attitude doesn't follow into his taste in artists."

"That's why he's being replaced." Jane shrugged. "We saw it coming. The Board wants to make money, and Mr. Storey insists on presenting a very traditional gallery. That just doesn't sell in today's market. The fact is that money is sexy, and people like to buy sexy and expensive things with it."

"Sarah Johnson has a lot of potential. I hate to see it wasted because of Milton."

"You've tried with her."

I frowned. "Not like I should've. I dismissed her practically from day one as his eye candy. If she didn't have such a great education I would've fired her already. And also, to be perfectly honest, I figured that Milton would be easier to manage if I kept her around."

Jane nodded after a moment. "Okay, but what about her attitude?"

"Well, I was quite full of myself at twenty-five."

"Yeah." Jane grinned and sat back in her chair. "Me, too."

The cute-ass guy returned with our food and refilled our drinks. We both watched him walk away before getting to our food. We ate mostly in silence; I suppose both of us were caught up in our own thoughts. Then rather unexpectedly, Jane stopped eating and cleared her throat. I barely had time to look around before Shamus Montgomery pulled out a chair and sat down at our table.

"Shame." I set my fork down. I fought the urge to lean closer. The man smelled like heaven.

He looked between us. "Hello, ladies. I just stopped by to get some takeout."

Jane offered him a smile. "Mercy tells me she's enjoying working with you."

I glared at her. I had said no such thing. "Actually, Jane was just telling me that she would love to pose for you."

Jane blushed. As far as I knew, she was one of the most modest women on earth. She had quit going to the gym because changing clothes in public freaked her out. I almost felt bad for saying what I did.

Shame looked over her face, then reached out and tilted her chin a little. "You have a strong face, Jane."

When he released her, she sucked in air and dropped both hands into her lap. "Thank you."

He turned to me. "You shouldn't pick on her, Mercy."

I laughed, and Jane let out a breath, realizing that he wasn't going to pursue her as a model. I responded, "She gets what she gives."

Shame stood and looked toward the cashier. "I'll see you tomorrow, Mercy."

Jane waited until he'd left the café before speaking. "Yep, he'll see *all* of you tomorrow."

I picked up my fork and stabbed a piece of chicken savagely. "It doesn't matter, it's like I'm not even real when I'm sitting in that chair."

"That sounds like a complaint."

It wasn't necessarily a complaint, but a part of me was hurt that he hadn't made a more serious play for me. Did I want to be in Shamus's bed? The answer was yes, of course. Not only did I want it, I expected it. Lust was turning deep circles in my body, heating at the mere thought of him.

Realizing that I hadn't responded to Jane, I shrugged and focused on my food.

I closed my door on Jerry and shut my eyes tightly. The man had actually thought that he was going to get invited in. Dinner had been dignified and very boring. How he thought such an event would translate into sex on the first date was beyond me.

In fact, as I turned and locked my door, I tried to remember the last time I'd actually ended up in bed with a man on a first date. Probably some time in college, when sex had been on my mind more often than not. Sex had always been something of a staple in my life. At least, until I'd been attacked.

That reminded me that I had homework to do for my therapist. Disgruntled, I checked my watch and sighed when I realized it wasn't even nine o'clock yet. If that wasn't a sign that the date had been bad, I don't know what was.

I walked to my answering machine and found the message light blinking. Ignoring it was tempting, but cowardly. I can't stand to be a coward. I pushed the "play" button with a jab of my finger and glared at the machine.

"Hey, I hope your date wasn't a snorefest." Jane sighed. "You know I hate this thing. Anyways, give me a call when you get back from Montgomery's tomorrow, and I expect some serious details."

I laughed and hit the "delete" button, then waited for the next message. It was a hang-up, which I erased. Changing my number was a damned pain in the ass. I hated having to do it, and this time I would have to change my cell phone number as well.

In my bedroom, I sat down at my desk and opened up my e-mail program. Maybe e-mailing my homework would be easier than having to discuss it in therapy. I opened a new e-mail message, hammered out my thoughts quickly, and hit "send." Since it was cowardly, I sat there for a few minutes after I'd done it, trying to decide what Lesley's response would be. I didn't have a session with her until Tuesday so I figured I was safe for the time being.

I stood and went into my closet to find something more comfortable to wear. I'd managed to pull a T-shirt on when the phone started to ring. Grabbing a pair of sweatpants, I went out in my bedroom and picked up the phone beside my bed.

"Hello."

"Hey."

I frowned and sat down on the bed. "Lisa."

"You pissed about the paint gun?"

I laughed softly. "No. I sort of expected it."

She sighed in my ear, and then I heard her breath catch. "This is going to sound crazy."

"I've come to expect the unexpected from you."

"I need you to come out here."

I frowned. As far as I could remember, she'd never invited me to her house. In fact, I normally had to press her several times for appointments, a task that I sort of viewed as entertainment.

"Are you all right?"

"No. I'm not."

"I'll be there as soon as I can." My grip tightened on the phone. "Can I bring anything?"

"No," she whispered.

The drive out to her farm house felt like a hundred years. When I turned down her driveway, dread pooled in my stomach. Every light in the sixty-year-old house was on. I threw my car in park and exited quickly. The front door was standing wide open, and when I came to it I realized that Lisa was sitting on her couch, with a gun across her lap.

Something told me that it wasn't her paint gun.

"Lisa."

She jerked and set aside the gun. "Mercy."

I went inside. To settle myself I took my time closing and locking the door. "What is wrong?"

She picked up a bottle of vodka that I hadn't noticed and took a healthy swig. "That son of a bitch ex-husband of mine."

I went to the couch, picked up the gun, and with ignorant if careful hands, moved it to the other side of the room and put it on a desk. "I often hear that about ex-husbands. I'm glad I don't have one."

"He called me," she whispered as if a part of her couldn't actually believed it had happened.

"The bastard."

"Exactly!" She hugged her bottle to her chest.

"So how long have you been drinking?"

"About two minutes."

"So, you aren't wasted?"

"Oh, Mercy." She sighed. "I'm wasted in so many ways. I'm wasted with regret and anger that I gave that man so much of my life. I'm wasted with desperation—that desperation I've carried in me since he hit me the first time."

"Your marriage has been over for years."

"My marriage was over that day. That day, today."

"What?" I turned and looked at her with a frown. "Are you sure you aren't drunk?"

She held up the bottle of vodka, which was nearly full, and then took a deep swallow. "Today is the ten-year anniversary of the death of my self-respect and my marriage."

"I don't understand."

"Today is the anniversary of the first time my husband hit me. The first time I let him get away with it."

I reached out and took the bottle. The vodka was sharp and smooth on my tongue. "Okay, this day officially sucks."

"I'd always said that a woman who stays with a man that

would hit her is pathetic. I promised myself I wouldn't be that woman."

"You loved him." I took another swallow before she took the bottle. Since I figured she'd needed it, I didn't protest.

"Yeah, I did. Loved him, thought I could change him. I seriously thought that if I could make him understand how much I loved him that it would be all right."

"So, what's up with the gun?"

"I thought he might come here."

"Why did he call?"

"I refused delivery of his last two support checks." She pursed her lips. "I can't live with taking his money anymore, and with the show just around the corner, I figure I don't have to."

"You'll be a very wealthy woman in a few weeks."

"Yes. I've already gotten offers." She laughed and shrugged. "I told them to contact you."

"Some people have. So, he wanted to know why you refused his checks."

"Yes." She frowned and sighed. "And I foolishly told him."

"You wanted to brag."

"Fuck." Lisa sat the bottle down and stood up. "Hell, yes, I wanted to brag. That bastard held me under his thumb for years. I couldn't work, so I never had the money to leave."

"Couldn't work?"

"He sabotaged every job I had. Made it impossible for me to have friends. Then one day I was standing the bathroom of his house with a pregnancy test in my hand."

"There was a baby?"

"No." She shook her head. "Just a scare. After the first year of our marriage, I realized that I didn't want to have children. I scrounged money from the grocery and household accounts to pay for birth control. He had no idea."

"He wanted children."

"He wanted another way to tie me up in his life." She motioned toward the kitchen. "I have some glasses to drink from."

I followed her into the kitchen and sat down in front of her while she poured me a generous drink. "I haven't had hard liquor in quite a while."

Lisa laughed softly. "Yeah, you do look like the wine type."

I cupped the glass in both of my hands. "So, he called."

"Yeah, he called. Today."

"Why today?"

"In our divorce papers, I gave the court only one date where he hit me."

"Today."

"Yes."

"Why?"

"Because that's the day he broke our marriage. It just took me five years to figure that out. I stood in front of that judge and told him I was a fool and an idiot. I didn't even want spousal support, but the judge understood something I didn't."

"What's that?"

"Greg made my life hell. That judge knew that getting a divorce from him wouldn't heal all of my wounds. When I bought this house, I spent six months here. Never leaving. I had groceries delivered and had the security system installed." She emptied her glass and grabbed the bottle. "Did you know I have proximity alarms? I know when a fucking car turns down my driveway."

"Have you seen a therapist?"

Lisa sat back in her chair. "I had a therapist coming out here. The last day she said she was wasting her time. Then she said I should call her when I was ready to actually start getting over the bastard."

"She thought you were still in love with him?"

"Yeah, little does she know that I plot his murder every morning in my shower."

I grabbed the bottle when she reached for it and set it away from her. "I think you've had enough."

"It usually takes the whole bottle."

"Well, let's pretend we drank it." I took her glass and stood from the table. "Have you eaten today?"

"Sure. Sometime, probably." She shrugged and glanced toward the bottle.

I walked back to the table and grabbed the bottle. "The man has turned you into a vicious and militant recluse. Don't let him turn you into an alcoholic, too."

"I'm not vicious."

"You shot one of my buyers with a paintball gun. Hell, you've shot me with a paintball gun."

"I gave you both fair warning." She crossed her arms over her breasts and glared at the table in front of her. "I had toast and coffee for breakfast."

I'd figured as much. I went to a pantry just off the kitchen and grabbed a loaf of bread. "I'll make you a sandwich."

"You weren't with Shame tonight."

"No." I came out and went to the refrigerator. "I had a date."

"Oh, yeah, Nerd of the Month."

"That's it. Both you and Jane are grounded and forbidden from speaking to each other."

Lisa laughed softly and rubbed her face. "She's a good lady, you're very lucky to have her at the gallery."

"I know." I grabbed some cheese and sandwich meat and took it all to the table.

"You were raped."

I paused and cleared my throat. "Yes."

"Did you fight back?"

"Not as much as I'd always thought I would. Before that night, I would've told anyone that a man would have to kill me to rape me. But I was so devastated by it that I could barely think, much less fight."

"He wasn't a stranger."

"No."

"The bastard."

"Yes." I nodded. "How long have you suspected?"

"Since our first conversation that didn't end with me shooting you with my paint gun." Lisa shrugged and sighed. "If I ever decide to kill Greg, I'll call you and get his name. If I'm going to go to prison, I might as well take out as many bastards as I can."

"How do you know he isn't in jail?" I put the plate with the sandwich on table in front of her and then set about fixing myself one.

She shrugged. "I just assumed. Bastards just seem to come out on top."

"Well, you assumed correctly." I sat down in front of her and took a bite of my sandwich. I seriously hoped that the food calmed my stomach. "So, my date was horrible."

"I would assume so." She stood up, walked to the pantry, and came back with a large bag of chips. "You were home early."

"How did you know I wasn't with Shame?"

"I called his place looking for you. He said you had a date and had cancelled tonight's session."

"He sounded put out about it, didn't he?"

"Shamus Montgomery doesn't like to share." She opened the bag, dumped some chips on her plate, and then laid the bag on the table in front of us. "So, yes, he sounded irritated."

"I'm not involved with that man on a personal level." When exactly had I become a bald-faced liar? Heat swept up my face when I glanced up and found her looking at me. "I mean it."

"Yeah, right."

"Look, he may be talented and sexy, but that doesn't mean

I'm going to fall at the man's feet. I have more dignity than that."

"Admitting that you want a man isn't a weakness."

I took another bite of my sandwich. "You aren't one to criticize."

"Yeah I know." She shrugged. "Well, from one dysfunctional woman to another . . . you could do a lot worse than follow Shame Montgomery into his bed."

"You've slept with him."

"Yes, some years ago, when we were both young and full of artistic snobbery, we dabbled in bed."

"Dabbled in bed."

"Okay, we had fine, hot jungle sex for about six months."

"And you are just friends now?"

"Yes, and have been for about ten years. We are both too old to play sex games. Nevertheless, it was fun then." She smiled and then chuckled. "A lot of fun."

"I don't want to hear about the sex you had with Shame."

"Ha, as if I'd sully the memory of it by sharing it." She grinned then. "He really is beautiful, though."

"Yes."

"And for the record . . . he has none."

"None of what?"

"Shame."

I turned over and punched at the pillow under my head. Lisa's guest room was nicely decorated. It had surprised me because I sort of expected a cot in a room full of boxes. I could hear her moving around in the room next to me. I knew that she wouldn't be sleeping any time soon.

I'd always expected that her marriage had been rough, I just honestly hadn't thought it involved physical abuse. It certainly explained her militant behavior about her space and her privacy.

CHAPTER 6

Shame was putting up a new display when I arrived. I locked the door and jingled the key he'd left in the slot as I walked toward him. He looked perfectly delicious, and I was certainly hungry. I'd overslept, so food was also on my mind. I'd slipped out of Lisa's house before she'd woke, mostly because I figured she would prefer it.

He offered me a smile and then finished arranging the smooth rosewood sculpture of woman and infant on the platform. "This has already been sold. But I couldn't resist displaying it for the few weeks that it will remain with me."

"It's beautiful." I walked to it and ran my hand along the sleek lines of the figures. The female figure emerged from the wood beautifully, and the infant was cradled close in her arms. "A commission?"

"Yes. A friend from college sent a picture of his wife and child to me and asked me if I could work with the picture. This is what I eventually came up with. I'll be shipping it to him in a few weeks. He's currently out of town on business."

"A surprise?"

"Yes. A good one, I hope."

"I couldn't imagine her not being pleased." I touched the infant's face with one fingertip. "A girl?"

"Yes. The wife is Lily, and the child is Abigail."

"It's beautiful, and probably worth a fortune."

Shame laughed softly. "Yes, I did warn Greg that he should refrain from mentioning where it came from."

"Does it bother you being so sought after?"

"At times. I don't regret the success I've had. It'd be rather difficult to. I'm able to support my grandparents and parents in a way that I've always wanted, and I'm doing something I love."

"And being fawned over by beautiful women is a fringe benefit."

He shot a glance my way and shrugged. "Yeah, something like that."

I frowned and then looked away. *Jealous over a man that I barely knew?*

"Are you ready to go above?"

"Yes." I still had his key. I offered it to him. His fingers brushed against mine as he took the key. I watched it disappear into the pocket of the loose linen pants he was wearing.

He looked so comfortable, I had the urge to pull the string on his pants and get him naked. Totally, completely naked. I went ahead of him up the stairs. The red chair was still in place. I wondered what he had planned for me. Walking toward the chair, I turned back to him.

"Well?"

"Let's get some breakfast."

I watched him walk toward the second set of stairs and raised an eyebrow. "Are you inviting me upstairs, Shame?"

He turned and looked me over. "It appears that I am."

I dropped my purse in the chair and followed along after him. The loft space that served as his residence was open and furnished in groupings. A profoundly large television took up one section on the opposite side of a stone fireplace. His kitchen was also open, with a cooking island.

"So, how was your date last night?"

I pursed my lips to keep from telling him the truth. "It was fine."

Shame laughed as he set out the eggs. "French toast?"

"Yeah." I slipped up onto the stool. "Do you need me to do anything?"

"No." He shook his head.

"Why did you laugh?"

"*Fine* is about the last term I'd ever want a woman to use when describing a date with me."

"It was a perfectly nice evening."

"Christ, Mercy, shut up before the cosmos opens up and destroys the poor man in absentia." He looked toward me. "Please tell me you didn't tell him you had a nice time."

I winced and shrugged. "I did."

"I'm never dating you."

I laughed and inclined my head as I looked him over. "What makes you think I'd want to date you anyway?"

Grinning, he pulled out a loaf of Texas toast bread and started cracking eggs into a bowl. "Get the cinnamon. It's in that spice rack over there."

I went and retrieved the cinnamon. "I met him at a speed-dating lunch."

"You don't strike me as the type of woman who has to re-sort to those kinds of things to get a man's attention."

I handed him the spice and went back to my place at the counter. "At any rate, it was uneventful."

"Lisa Millhouse called here looking for you."

"Yes." I nodded and looked up to find him staring. "I sup-pose you know she was upset."

"Yes. I offered to come out and sit with her, but I got the impression that my dick made me less-than-desirable com-pany."

"Her house is definitely a dick-free zone." I watched him open the refrigerator and pull out a couple of bottles of water. I took one he offered. "I spent the night at her place."

"The two of you don't appear to have a lot in common."

"Appearances can be deceiving." I watched him maneuver bread into the frying pan in front of him. "She is a strong and thoughtful woman. I find her rather stimulating to be around."

"You should have known her before she married Greg Carson." He shook his head. "She was a wild and carefree woman. Had a smile for everyone and anyone. Couldn't meet a stranger."

"How well do you know her ex-husband?"

"Well enough to want to put my fist through his face." He glanced back at me. "He's a poor excuse for a man and a human being."

"From what I've heard I can only agree." I rolled the bottle of water between my hands. "You and she were lovers."

"Yes, in college. I could hardly resist her."

I smiled at his rueful tone. "So why didn't the two of you end up together?"

"We had sex and art in common. It didn't take us long to realize that was just about it. Still, I consider my relationship with her one of my best. She taught me a lot about women."

"She thinks you're beautiful."

"I think the same of her." He went to a cabinet and pulled out some plates. "I'm surprised she discussed our past with you."

"It just came up." I frowned.

"My sexual relationship with Lisa Millhouse just came up?" He raised one eyebrow. "Mercy, are you keeping something from me?"

"Women discuss a lot of things. There is no rhyme or reason to it."

Having eaten my way through four slices of French toast, I found myself once more confronted with the chair. I turned to him. "Where do you want me?"

"The possible answers to that question boggle the mind." He motioned at the chair. "Undress."

I unbuttoned the front of my sundress and slipped it off my shoulders. Carrying it to the dressing screen, I tossed it across the top, and pushed off my shoes. Turning, I hooked my fingers into the small pair of cotton panties I still wore.

"Leave them on." I fought the urge to cover my breasts as I walked to the chair. Why was I still so nervous? The man had seen everything I had. He'd also touched me in the most intimate way possible, even if the touch had been fleeting.

I sat down in the chair and looked toward the alabaster. It was a different shape now, with a defined, nearly square, bottom. The part that would eventually be me was shaped.

"Pull your legs up like you did last time." He squatted down in front of me as I did what he as he said, "Good, now bring the arms around just as before."

"Why like this?"

"Your modesty is appealing and honest." He pushed my hair off my shoulders and lifted my chin slightly. "Just like that. Let me know when you need a break."

"Okay."

I watched him pull on safety goggles and go to work. He focused, and after a while, it was as if I wasn't even there. I'd been around art most of my life, knew more artists than other kinds of people. Still, watching him work was a unique experience for me. It was the first time I'd ever watched an artist work.

He stopped and looked at me. "Take off the panties."

I flushed and let my legs go. Looking to him, I stood up from the chair. "Why?"

He pulled his safety goggles into place and watched as I did as he had requested. Glaring at him because he hadn't answered my question, I slipped back into the chair and pulled my legs back up. I felt the difference, the vulnerability. I glanced in his direction and found him nodding. With a blush staining my face and neck, I placed my arms back around my legs as he'd positioned them.

"Tell me about your first sexual experience."

I jumped a little, startled by his words, and made myself meet his gaze, my mouth dry. "I'd rather not."

He chuckled. "Tell me anyway."

I refused to meet his eyes. "I was sixteen."

"Not a good experience, I take it." He didn't look to me as he spoke. "Tell me about your first real lover."

My thoughts drifted to the young man I'd known in college. "It was in college. We were friends until the night we went to bed together. We were lovers until he graduated."

"You enjoyed him?"

"Yes." I had. Brian was a very good memory. "He had good hands and gave effortlessly in bed. He was the first man I'd ever been with where I was interested in his pleasure. He taught me a great deal about being a good lover."

"Do you have a lover now, Mercy?"

"Not at the moment." I wasn't surprised by the question. I was, however, irritated that I had answered it so quickly.

"Why?"

I glared at him. "That is none of your business."

Shame paused briefly and nodded as he went back to work. "Tell me, do you enjoy a woman in your bed as much as a man?"

"I've never been with a woman." However, the thought had crossed my mind a time or two. I didn't think I would ever sleep with a woman, but there was something about that taboo that I found interesting.

"But you'd like to."

I flushed and lowered my gaze back to the floor. "I didn't say that."

When I looked up at him, he was concentrating once more

on the area he was working with a thin chisel. I asked him, "Have you ever been with another man?"

"No." He picked up a cloth from the floor and used it to clear away dust and particles. "I have a friend who'll fuck anything that will sit still long enough, but I prefer women."

"Anything?"

He shrugged. "I haven't seen him make an exception yet."

"I've known several straight men that wouldn't be comfortable with a bisexual friend."

"Derek isn't bisexual. He's trisexual."

"Trisexual?"

Shame laughed. "He'll try anything once. As for his attraction to men, it doesn't bother me. He knows he'll get nowhere fast with me." He frowned, looking at the work he had done and toward my hands. "You have nice hands."

"Thanks." They were my grandmother's hands. I'd noticed that fact a few years ago when I'd bought myself a rather amazing diamond for my birthday. The ring was still one of my favorites.

"What do you like about sex?"

I took a deep breath. "Why do you insist on asking me such personal questions?"

"You are in my favorite chair, naked."

Well, I was naked. I wondered why he was using the chair. Finding myself naked in his favorite piece of furniture felt odd and intimate. Just as intimate as that moment when he'd slipped his fingers into me. I clenched my thighs briefly as the memory stirred my body.

What could it hurt to answer his questions? "I like being close to someone. Just touching and being touched is good. There is something beautiful about those first moments of discovery."

"Yet your bed is empty."

Once more, I found myself looking at the floor that

stretched out between us. There was nothing I could say that wouldn't reveal what had been taken me from in New York. It wasn't something I talked about casually. Sitting up a little straighter, I didn't say anything. I wasn't going to let him bait me into giving him information about my past.

"I heard you are courting Samuel Castlemen for this winter?" Shame asked.

Relieved that he'd changed the subject, I sighed. "Yes. I'd like to bring his *Phases of a Woman* to Boston. He put me off for a while, but he e-mailed me because he'd heard that you were going to show with the gallery. So I owe you my thanks." I was relieved that he'd decided to change the subject. I took a deep breath and willed my stomach to stop jumping.

"He's a talented man. The power he can put on canvas is something to be envied." He pulled off his protective goggles and laid them aside. "You need a break; you've been sitting like that for an hour and a half."

I let my arms fall to my side, surprised so much time had passed. "Are you ready to stop?"

"I'm at a good place to stop." Shame stopped a foot away from me and looked me over. "Are you ready to stop?"

"Stop what?" I asked. I was really ready to stop playing his game, but I didn't know if that was what he meant.

"Hiding."

"You've seen and *touched* more of me than any man I've dated in recent memory. I fail to see what I could be hiding."

His gaze dropped briefly to my breasts, and a smile moved across his lips briefly before he met my gaze. "You've been dating some profoundly unlucky men." He took a step closer. "Why are these men so unlucky?"

They were all boring men that I'd chosen to go out with because I wasn't interested in fucking them. Of course, telling Shame that was out of the question. I pulled my legs back up and wrapped my arms around them. "You're getting very personal with me, Shamus."

"And if I told you I wanted to get as personal as possible with you?" He moved around the chair, and his fingers trailed along the back, catching in my hair briefly. "How would you feel about that?"

"That depends." I flushed a little, remembering the feel of his hand cupping my sex, a finger sliding between my labia.

"On what?"

"Do you want more from me than the occasional fuck?"

"I am a man of some appetite. So we can say that it wouldn't be just an occasional fuck."

"Okay . . . so do you want more than to fuck me regularly?" I smiled briefly when he came back around in front of me. "Our physical attraction is there, but I'm too old to play such games."

It was obvious that our conversation was affecting him as much as it was me. I pressed my thighs together in an effort to ignore the stinging arousal that burned there. My gaze flicked back to his face before dropping to the tented fabric of his pants. I was seriously interested in seeing how big his cock was. I had a feeling I wouldn't be disappointed.

"I don't know you well enough to ask for a lot. I want you, and what I had the other night is simply not enough."

"Yeah. I noticed." I dropped my gaze to his crotch again and wet my lips.

The man was going to kill me with sexual frustration. I desperately wanted him to make a move, yet I knew somehow that he wouldn't. I also didn't think I was brave enough to ask for it. Some modern woman I'd turned out to be. I couldn't even tell a man I wanted to have sex with him. But it was more than sex. I needed more, and I wasn't sure I could accurately communicate that.

"It's rather unfair that your own state of arousal isn't more obvious."

My hands tightened briefly into fists and then I forced them to relax. I knew that I was soaking wet. All I had to do was release my legs and spread them. The damp curls that covered my sex would be obvious. My nipples tightened against my thighs as I considered what I should do. Carefully, I released my legs and let them slide to the floor. I sucked in a breath as I met his gaze. I could feel my nipples hardening further. They started to hurt.

His gaze was hard, tense. I could feel his tension moving between us. I spread my legs further and bit down on my lip as his gaze automatically dropped to my pussy. My thighs were damp, so I knew there would be no mistaking my physical state. I wanted him to drag me from the chair, toss me on the floor, and fuck me unconscious. I wasn't ready to ask.

I watched his tongue slip out and wet his bottom lip, and my thighs tensed in response. I only had to ask. If I asked, he would come to me and slip that tongue in and eat me. I knew it and I wanted it.

"You could drive a man insane like that." He took a step back from me and the space he'd given me in his favorite chair. "Padded walls and a straitjacket insane."

I scooted forward in the chair and planted my feet flat on the floor. "You want me."

"Of course."

I ran my hands down my thighs and stretched a little. "But?"

"But I don't take advantage of women."

"You think you'd be taking advantage of me?"

"You aren't here of your own free will. You're naked in my studio because I outmaneuvered you. So yes, I'd be taking advantage of you." I watched him swallow hard and close his eyes briefly. "I won't be that kind of man."

"I understand."

He offered me his hand and I accepted it without thinking. Standing in front of him, I cleared my throat. "Shame?"

"Yes, Mercy?"

"I should probably get dressed." I moved past him, resisting the urge to brush against him, and went behind the screen.

With unsteady hands, I pulled my dress off the screen and put it back on. Once the top of it was laced closed, I went back around the screen for my shoes. Shamus was sitting in the red chair watching me. I asked him, "Why did you kiss me the other day?"

He didn't answer immediately. After what seemed a long time he looked at me. "I couldn't help myself. I have little impulse control when it comes to you, it seems. At the time you didn't seem to mind. Did I upset you?"

"No." I picked up my purse and rummaged through it for my keys. "I was just surprised."

"You are a beautiful woman, Mercy. It shouldn't be a surprise to you that men find you attractive."

I felt myself blush. How in the hell could I be blushing when I had just spread my legs wide for this man? "I was under the impression that you didn't date white women."

He laughed and leaned back in the chair. "I like women a lot, no matter their color. My own mother is only half black."

"You don't always act like a man who's attracted to me."

"I don't normally sleep with my models."

"You've said that before." I looked at him, saw the frustration and confusion on his face. I found that surprising. He hadn't struck me as a man who would easily display his thoughts.

"I can't think of you sexually while I work. I wouldn't get anything accomplished."

"You questioned me about my sex life."

"That was about making you uncomfortable."

His admission fell between us, and the silence stretched taut. "Why?"

"I want to capture what I see in you when no one is looking," he murmured.

"And what is that?"

"You aren't comfortable in your own skin."

I flushed with anger. "That's not true."

"Mercy, will you tell me why you left New York?"

My stomach knotted up again. The thought of revealing to him the ugliness of my past almost made me physically ill. This talented man who had kissed me because he couldn't help himself didn't deserve the extent of my nightmare. I straightened my shoulders and glanced toward the stairs that functioned as my escape route.

"I've already told you."

"You told me a half-truth." He reached out to touch me. His fingers were warm and soft as they moved across my cheek and traveled with a fleeting motion over my lips. "I see the fear."

I backed away, angry at the invasion. Deep down I knew that my anger was irrational, but I couldn't help it. "I'm going to go."

"I'll see you Monday."

I nodded. At the stairs, he called my name. I turned to look at him. "Yes, Shame?"

"Why did you kiss me back?"

I looked over his face and smiled. "I couldn't help myself."

At home, I stripped off my clothes in my living room and went naked to the bathroom. I'd always found being naked a liberating and relieving experience. It's as if my whole body can relax and breathe. I thought about Shamus, and knew that my reactions to him were different. In fact, being naked with Shame wasn't like anything I'd ever known. The lovers of my past were pale, thin ghosts compared with the solid and real form of Shamus Montgomery.

I looked in the mirror and took in my breasts, full C cups, still firm and high. My nipples were pink but grew darker when aroused. I had a decent stomach for my size, not flat but certainly not flabby. I had full hips, decent thighs, and an ass that I wouldn't have wished on my worst enemy. Well, maybe I would. I checked it out in the mirror and sighed.

After taking a quick shower, I grabbed a snack and sat down in front of the television. Three hours of channel surfing later, all I could say with complete honesty was that I was absolutely sick of real people. I went to my bedroom and took out my favorite vibrator. It was sleek, with a rotating head and a little latex thing that stimulated my clit when I inserted it in my pussy.

It couldn't replace the warm glide of a man between my legs, but as substitutions went, it wasn't bad. I pulled off the T-shirt and shorts I'd tugged on after my shower and slipped into my bed. Turning on the vibrator, I slid it between my labia gently. The hum of the vibrator itself was enough to make me wet, and having it pressed against my clit brought arousal rushing to the surface.

Pushing it inside, I pressed the button that controlled the clit stimulator. My body responded instantly to the quick pleasure of the mechanical device. Heat flushed over my body as I thought about Shame and his hands. It would be so good to have him touch and stroke me the way he had the alabaster as he'd worked on the sculpture. With my free hand, I fondled one breast, pinching and pulling at the nipple until it hurt.

The heat of orgasm took my breath as it moved over my body. It was so much pleasure that it almost hurt. Pulling the vibrator out of my pussy, I tossed it on the bed beside me. My clit was throbbing pleasantly between my labia.

I had masturbated for as long as I could remember. Staring at the ceiling, I thought about the pleasure I could attain alone, and the pleasure of being with a man. Two years was a long time to go without a man. I had kept my bed empty on purpose, and the reasons were twofold. Flushing with anger, I stood from the bed and took the vibrator to the bathroom.

I washed it and laid it on a hand towel on the bathroom

counter. It was too late to push the memory back. It was there, already in the front of my mind, devastating and so harsh that I could almost smell Jeff. Running my finger along my jaw, I could still remember the horror and pain of that moment. He'd hit me only once. I'd been so stunned, so hurt that I'd given Jeff my trust.

Dropping my hand from my face, I went into the bedroom and tried to forget him. It was no use. Frustrated and getting angrier by the minute, I went to the kitchen and pulled a bottle of Crown Royal out of the freezer. I liked my whiskey cold. I poured half a glass and leaned against the counter while I drank it.

Alcohol did nothing to soothe me, it never had. I finished off the glass and waited for the numbness to set in. Drinking didn't push the memories away, but it made remembering easier to handle. I wondered briefly what it did for Lisa. Did it push it all away, or did it make her feel strong enough to stand up to the man who'd beat her?

Jeff had broken my trust, taken it from me when I'd begged him not to. Hurt me, raped me, and pretended all the while that I wanted it. I was ashamed of that night in a way that I could barely put into words. Ashamed that I had trusted him, and so hurt that he hadn't deserved it. I'd quit my job at the museum when I found I couldn't enter the building without wanting to curl up and die. I never wanted to see him again.

Thinking about that horrible night inevitably brought to mind the person who'd found me, Martin, the sweetest and most thoughtful man I'd ever known. He'd found me huddled in my office the next morning, where Jeff King had left me, broken and savaged with emotional and physical trauma. Martin had picked me up off the floor and carried me to the couch in his office. Then he'd talked me into going to the emergency room.

I remember the two detectives, the man with the face that

showed he'd known too many tragedies, and the woman who desperately wanted to help me heal, who had come to collect my rape kit. They'd been disappointed when I told them that there would be no charges filed and that I would not name the man responsible. In the end, Martin had asked them to leave and abide by my decision. The woman had lingered at the door. As she turned to leave, I saw tears streaming down her face.

She'd never seemed to understand the choice I made that night. She had cried for me. I hadn't cried, and that thought lingered with me for months after I moved to Boston. I had survived Jeff, and that had always been enough, until now.

My thoughts drifted to Shamus Montgomery and his beautiful work. His passion for life and art was a part of who he was, and I feared exposing him to all that I was. I wouldn't taint him with my memories of Jeff. Unwillingly, a mental picture of Lisa Millhouse's last work came to me. I saw the woman, her femininity bared before the world, hovering at the feet of some unknown and evil force.

Shaken, I walked to the phone and picked it up. Dialing Lisa's number from memory, I spoke the moment she answered the phone. "Is it me?"

Silence lingered and then Lisa spoke. "It's both of us, Mercy."

"You've known for months, how?" I demanded softly.

"Looking in your face was like looking in a mirror." I heard her sigh, and then she continued. "Are you afraid to go to sleep at night?"

"Only on nights like this." I walked through my house and sat down on the couch. "You?"

"It comes and goes for me. Is it Shamus?"

"I don't understand what you mean."

"You do," Lisa responded. "You're attracted to him."

"Yes."

"You want him." She sounded amused.

"Yes."

"Almost to the point of painful violence, and you wonder if you are sick for thinking that way."

I closed my eyes. "Christ, Lisa." Lisa laughed, and I could hear her moving around. "What are you doing?"

"Making a sandwich. You woke me, and now I'm hungry."

I was sorry that I'd woken her, but found myself unwilling to end the call. "It's a little early in the evening to be asleep."

Lisa snorted. "I take it when I can get it. Does Shame make you nervous?"

"I'm not afraid of him."

"No, I know you aren't."

"I have too much baggage to have a relationship with a man like him."

"He's a man. Yes, he is a passionate and sensitive artist, but he's also a strong and caring man. Shamus is a thoughtful and thorough lover. If he is interested in you, and I'm surprised, considering his own rules about his models, then it's because he sees something special and lovely in you."

"I'm way too messed up to be involved with a man like him. He deserves better."

"That's bullshit. What happened to you doesn't make you less than what you were before."

I sighed. "He's too much for me."

"He's a good man, Mercy. You can trust him."

"I do."

"And it scares you."

I groaned. "I never realized you were psychic."

"It's a hidden talent." Lisa paused and then grunted. "We didn't discuss that woman last night. I understand why you couldn't warn me ahead of time that she was coming out here, but, I swear, things are going to get nasty if she gets brave enough to try it again."

"I have to pick and choose my battles until August," I

finally said. "I know that makes me sound like a coward, but Milton Storey is up to something, and I considered his interference on your account a small thing compared with whatever else he might have planned."

"I could kill him and bronze him for you. He'd make a horrid but interesting garden gnome."

I laughed aloud. "Thanks, I'll keep that in mind."

"I've been thinking about the high-school art project. I think that's great, you can count me in for it."

"Oh, thanks. Jane is proud of it. I'm glad the Board agreed with me. Have you told her, yet, that you'll be part of it?"

"No, I'm still plotting young Sarah's downfall. I'll give Jane a call." She paused and sighed. "Thanks for last night."

"We all need something or someone every now and again."

After my phone call ended, I spent several hours in front of the television and then went to bed. Lying there, I thought about Martin again. He'd been my close and soothing friend after the attack. It had been no surprise to me when, two months after my rape, I sought his physical comfort. The sex hadn't been mindblowing, but it had done a lot to heal the damage that had been done. When I'd decided to leave New York and Martin, he hadn't tried to hold me back or change my mind.

He had gone to great lengths to make the decision painless. He'd helped me sell my apartment and what furniture I wasn't going to take with me. I valued him for the dear friend he was, but a part of me still hurt for the pain I caused him. It wasn't until after I'd left New York that I realized how much Martin loved me and how hurt he'd been when I decided to leave. It had been too late to take that decision back, and though our friendship was different, I still counted him among my closest friends.

The wedding invitation was still on my kitchen table. He'd found a woman he couldn't live without and planned to marry her. I was happy for him, but there was another part of me that had been devastated by that knowledge. He was no longer there to fall back on, to depend on. I felt selfish and mean for it.

Martin was the second reason my bed had been empty for two years. I'd used him, and I'd promised myself that I wouldn't do that to another man.

CHAPTER 7

I spent the whole day thinking about what I wanted and needed, and by the time I arrived at Shame's gallery at 5:30 PM, I wasn't exactly sure what I was going to do. Calling him and inviting myself over had probably been one of the boldest things I'd done in recent memory. Since I hadn't given him much of a chance to respond to my request to come over, I was very unsure of my reception.

I entered the gallery and glanced around. Shame was at his desk with a customer. He looked in my direction and nodded. I unhooked the PRIVACY sign and then hooked it back into place before I went up the stairs. Once in his studio, I walked toward the sculpture. I could make out the shape of me, my face, and the lower part of my legs. The arms were emerging, barely.

I reached out and touched the face of the sculpture. He still had work to do, but it was fascinating to look at that alabaster and see myself coming out of it. I'd been up there a few minutes when he appeared. He shut the door and pushed a set of keys into his pocket.

"You didn't have to close early because I arrived."

"I only opened for her. I don't normally keep any weekend hours."

He leaned on the door, silent and watchful. Then he pushed away from the door and walked toward me. The moment he could, he reached out for me. His hands were drifting over my face as he pulled me close and kissed me. I dropped my purse without hesitating and wrapped my arms around his neck.

Flush against the heat of him, I was breathless with wonder and something so hot and bone twisting I could barely recognize it. Desire, lust, and pain mixed in my body as he lifted me off the floor and coaxed my legs around his waist. I wanted this man like hell, and I didn't care what the consequences were. My fingers dug into his shoulders as he pressed me against the wall.

Heat and ache followed his mouth as he kissed my neck and shoulder. Pushing the strap of my dress out of his way, his teeth nipped at my skin. One shuddering breath after another was wrenched from me as he ground his body against mine. With a sob of frustration, I arched against him. I'd never felt so empty in my life.

"Shame."

"I know, Mercy."

He pulled at my dress until my right breast was exposed. Sucking the nipple into his mouth, he held me tight. The pull of his mouth was overwhelmingly hot. I felt like I was going to burst out of my skin. Knowing what he needed to hear, I sucked in a deep breath.

"Shame. You have to fuck me. Now."

"God, Mercy, do you know what you are asking?"

"I'm not asking." His head jerked up and our gazes locked. "You have to fuck me right now."

His grip loosened on me and I let my legs drop to support me. Without another word, he slipped his hand into mine and pulled me toward the second set of stairs. I fought the urge to start undressing as we walked up.

Shamus pulled me across his living area quickly and then we went up the set of stairs that led to the third, partial level.

I could see most of the loft below as I paused there at the foot of the bed. The bed was low to the floor. I looked at him then, saw the hard passion I had for him mirrored in his eyes. This was our final step, the point of no return.

Pulling my dress over my head, I tossed it on the floor. I wasn't wearing a bra. My nipples were impossibly hard and aching. I rubbed them with the palms of my hands as he pulled his shirt free from his slacks and unbuttoned it hastily. Discarding my panties, I shoved them aside and crawled onto the bed. On my knees, I turned to face him as he undressed. He was beautiful, and so dark compared with me. The contrast of his skin and mine was such a turn-on that I had to close my eyes briefly. When I opened them, he had discarded both his pants and a pair of boxers. My eyes lingered on the boxers briefly, both surprised and amused.

"I take it you like the Tasmanian Devil?"

He laughed and glanced briefly at the cartoon-decorated boxers. "Yeah, I do."

My gaze traveled back to him, taking in the length and width of his erection. He had to be nine and a half inches—and so thick I'd barely be able to wrap my hand around him. Wetting my lips, I looked up to his face and rubbed my legs together as I lay back on the bed. "Come here, Shame."

He went to the nightstand and pulled out a box of condoms. I nodded my approval and held out my hand for him. Shamus came to me, sliding his body against mine and wrapping his arms around me. I loved the feel of him. The heat of his body warmed and excited my skin. He covered my mouth with his the moment he could.

The kiss was hot and passionate, full of as much longing as I had, and all the passion I hadn't fully realized he had for me. The knowledge that he wanted me was a heady and rewarding experience. He pulled his mouth from mine and lowered it to my breasts. He kissed and sucked my nipples until they were so rigid they hurt. All the while, his hands moved over my hips and ass, pulling me closer and pressing the full length of his cock against my stomach.

"Tell me how you want it, Mercy." He pressed a kiss against my stomach before allowing himself to go lower. Carefully he spread my legs. "Tell me."

I arched against his mouth as he nuzzled me and used his tongue to separate my labia. The tip of his tongue stabbed at my throbbing clit until I was twisting against him. "Put your cock in me, Shame."

"Hard?"

"Yes." I watched as he freed the black latex from the foil and rolled it into place. "Any way you want."

He spread my legs gently as he knelt between them. It was so sexy watching his dark hands move over my pale thighs. He pushed the head of his cock against my entrance and slid into me. With my back arched and my legs spread wider, I shuddered as he sank fully into me. *No longer empty*, I thought fleetingly as I met the thrust of his hips.

"Yes," I whispered, taking each invasion, my body demanding more.

I wrapped myself around his strength and let go. It had been so long since I'd trusted a man this way that I could barely hold on to my sanity. The hot penetration of his cock and his mouth drifting over mine were everything I needed. The pleasure of him was deep, and it twisted inside my body until I didn't know where we separated, or even if we could.

He slowed the stroke of his cock and lifted his head. Our eyes met and held. I was taken in by the passion he couldn't express and the need he didn't bother to hide. The way we fit together was perfect and almost painful in its honesty. Pressing fully into me, he ran one hand down my side and then up my leg.

"I want to be on top."

He laughed softly at my demand, but pulled from me to

oblige. I slid astride him and sank onto the length of his cock with a sigh of relief. A shudder ran down my back as I started to move. His hands moved over my thighs and to my hips, and he gripped me, teaching me the rhythm he wanted. The steady thrust of his body underneath me lifted us off the bed and forced my body to accept every glorious inch of him.

God, I loved a big cock. I let my head fall back as I moved with him. The naughty pleasure of fucking a man I barely knew was there, but there was also a feeling of connection and desire. This man knew me and my body in ways that I didn't even understand. He ran his thumbs along my labia as I rocked on him and teased my clit gently.

He hissed as the muscles of my pussy tightened against the pleasure and the building orgasm. "Perfect."

He sat up as I started to come, wrapped his arms around me, and rocked me gently as pleasure swept over me. I wrapped my arms around his neck and kissed him hard. Our tongues slid against each other, exploring that wet sensation as I continued to move on his cock.

"You have an amazing pussy."

I laughed and kissed his mouth gently. "If I'd known you had this big, thick cock to share, I would have jumped your bones sooner."

Running his hands down my back, he cupped my ass and ground against me. "We aren't finished."

"Oh, I know," I whispered against his mouth as I kissed his lips, pleased with the softness of them. His tongue darted against my lips and sought entry into my mouth.

I lost myself in the kiss as he rolled us over and put me on my back. Releasing my mouth, he started to move, each thrust measured and sure. My insides trembled with each thrust and each retreat. His body jerked briefly as he fought to keep from coming. Then he shortened his stroke and ground against me.

"Don't." I touched his face. "Come for me, Shamus. Don't hold back on me."

I took his face into both of my hands and made him keep his gaze on me as he thrust into me that final time. His body shook from the force of it. I watched him close his eyes, and then he lowered his body to mine. Bodies slick with sweat, we lay there, wrapped up in each other and shaking, for a long time. Finally, when we were still, he pulled from me and rolled onto his back.

"The first time I saw you, it was in New York. You were in the museum talking to Edward Morrison. Did you know you talk with your hands?"

I laughed softly. "Sometimes I even do it when I'm on the phone."

"I had a meeting to get to, so I couldn't stop to meet you. When I went back and talked to Edward, he told me that you were leaving New York and he had no idea where you were going. Six months ago, I was at an auction looking to buy back a piece I'd sold when I was starting out. You were there, bidding on it. I got so flustered looking at you, I lost the auction to you."

I had the grace to blush at that. "I was determined to get it. I didn't see you there."

"I had someone standing on the floor for me. I was in a private room. I forgot about my buyer." He placed a soft kiss on my shoulder. "I should probably do some work."

I nodded. "I could use a shower before we get started."

"Sounds like fun."

I left the bed and glanced back at him briefly before I walked into the bathroom. I'd gotten exactly what I wanted, and it had been all that I could've hoped for. As a lover he was just as attentive and thoughtful as I'd hoped he would be.

His shower stall was as big as some bathrooms I'd seen, with three showerheads. By the time I had them turned on and adjusted the temperature just right, he joined me. He pulled me into his arms and kissed me gently. I wanted to tell him that he didn't need to be gentle with me, that I wasn't fragile. I loved the way his hands were moving softly and lightly over my skin.

I gasped a little as the foil of the condom in his hand scraped against the skin on my back. He tore the condom package open and tossed the wrapper over his shoulder. Taking the latex from him, I rolled it onto his cock, taking my time, despite the way his breathing hitched every time my fingers slid on him. I cupped his balls and massaged them carefully, his cock jerking between us.

When he could take no more, he pulled my hand from him and gathered me close. His mouth on mine, his hands roaming over my body, I started to shake with my need. I'd never wanted like this, never hurt for a man like this. The cool tile wall of the shower met with my back as Shamus picked me up and pushed into me. I arched against him and moaned.

I couldn't help the shudder that took over my body almost immediately. "God."

"Hmm." He sighed, and buried his face in my neck. His hands moved underneath me and cupped my ass to keep our position against the wall. "Well, He made me, but I'm the one doing the work here."

I laughed and closed my eyes. "And He made you so well." I tightened my legs around his waist and took a deep breath as he took his second stroke into me.

He lowered his head to my shoulder and made a tangled sound deep in his chest. "You're going to be sore for days."

Didn't I know it? His cock was so gloriously big. "I won't even be able to sit tomorrow without thinking about you being inside me."

He groaned and pushed deep into me again. "Good."

His next thrust into me was hard, and the relentless heat of it wrung several broken cries from me. Holding me high against the wall, he bared his teeth on my shoulder, scraping my skin as he started to thrust quick and hard. I loved it and moaned every time he buried himself fully into me.

"Are you going to come for me?"

I closed my eyes and bit down on my lip. The steady and relentless drive of his cock into me was like dying repeatedly. His flesh blended hot and full with my body.

I moaned a little and my whole body flushed with orgasm. "Oh, God."

"That's it, baby." He gripped me tightly against him. "Give in to me."

I came down the stairs wrapped in a towel, with my hair pinned up, as he'd requested as he'd left the shower. He was standing on the other side of the sculpture, staring at it. He looked every bit as aloof and professional as he had the first time I sat for him. He glanced toward me and then back to the sculpture as I took a seat in the chair and pulled my legs up into position. I was pleasantly sore. Muscles that I hadn't used in a while tingled under my skin.

I looked at him and found him staring. "Am I positioned wrong?"

He shook his head and sighed. "No. I thought that sleeping with you would take the edge off the piece, but it hasn't."

He went to work, leaving me with my thoughts. It had occurred to me after the shower that I should tell him about New York and why I had left there. Keeping it a secret didn't seem right in light of the change in our relationship.

I looked toward him and found him frowning. "What's wrong?"

"You don't look happy about this, Mercy."

"I've just got something difficult to tell you. I don't want to, but I don't think I can keep it from you and feel good about what we are developing here." I took a deep breath and focused on the floor in front of me. Why was it so hard?

"About New York," he said softly.

My gaze jerked to his and I sighed. "Yes, about New York." I took a deep breath. "You're the second man I've been with since I was raped."

"Raped." The word came out of his mouth hard and sounded so painful that I flinched.

I knew there was no word that was as hateful as rape. I nodded and watched a multitude of emotions cross his face. Anger and sadness were the only ones that lingered.

He cleared his throat and focused on the alabaster for a few moments, his hands still. "Thank you for trusting me."

"I do trust you." Unable to help myself, I started to talk. "His name was Jeff King. He worked at the museum with me. We were friends. Well, I thought we were friends. It wasn't the first time we'd worked past the closing of the museum. We were getting an exhibit together. I wanted to get it done early so I could go out of town for a long weekend."

I couldn't tell him about it. Only Lesley had heard all of the details, and it had taken me hours with her to get it all out. Disgruntled, I looked at him. "Martin found me, saved me in several ways, actually. I felt so lonely and broken. He helped me put the pieces back together."

"He fell in love with you."

I nodded. "Yes, I didn't realize that until later. Sex had always been about pleasure for me, at least before I was raped. Afterward, my feelings about sex were mixed. I knew that what had happened to me hadn't been about sex or desire, but I was uncomfortable around men who wanted me. Martin wasn't sexually aggressive; to be honest, I initiated all of our sexual encounters. One night I realized that I was using him. I felt sick about it. I made the decision to leave New York and Martin. I didn't deserve his friendship."

He was silent for a moment and then cleared his throat. "I need to think about this a while."

I nodded and tightened up my position so that he could

work. Shame was rather introspective, so I had expected him to back off a little while he digested what I had told him.

I stayed where I was for several hours as he worked. Moving, stretching, and standing when he suggested it. It was nearly midnight when he set down the tool he'd worked with and his gaze moved over my legs and hands. He frowned and then glanced at the clock on the wall.

"You should have let me know it was so late."

"You were in a good place." I stretched my legs out in front of me and lay back in the chair.

He came to me, his hands covered with dust from the alabaster, and knelt in front of the chair. I moved my legs as he ran his fingers along the back of my knees. The dust on his hands was rough, and the sensation was delicious.

"Your trust in me is amazing. Had I known that was what you hid, I'm not sure I would have manipulated you into posing for me." He cleared his throat. "Your presence and personality were challenging. I wanted to strip you down, get rid of all the social pretense we put in place for civility, so that I could see what you were really about."

"And now?"

"Now I am amazed that you trust me as much as you do."

Gently, he pulled me forward until I was sitting closer to the edge of the chair, and lifted one leg onto his shoulder. Then he lowered his head to me and slipped his tongue between my labia.

I fell back against the chair and curled my fingers into the armrests. I got so hot so fast that I could barely think. His tongue rushed warm and wet against my clit before slipping into me. The dipping motion of his tongue and the brush of his lips felt so perfect. I lifted my hips briefly and then sank back into the chair as Shame pressed two fingers into my cunt.

"Fuck." Closing my eyes, I forced myself to relax as his

lips closed gently over my clit. He used the tip of his tongue to lick and tease me.

I cried out when he lifted his head and stood.

Shame pulled me from the chair and guided me toward the stairs. Hot and mentally weak with lust, I went with him. Once more, I found myself at the foot of his bed, watching him undress. He rolled on a condom while I crawled up onto the bed and lay on my back. Running my hands over my thighs, I could already imagine him inside me.

"Come here," I demanded softly as I pulled my legs up and placed my feet flat on the mattress. "Now. I'm in no mood for play."

"Neither am I." He put one knee on the bed and inclined his head as he looked me over. "Get on your hands and knees."

Smiling, I sat up and then rolled to my knees. His hands skimmed down my back as he joined me on the bed and kissed my shoulder softly. I closed my eyes and curled my hands into the sheets as he pressed me gently into position. His cock brushed between my thighs, and I got wetter. Widening my legs, I arched a little and groaned when the head of his cock brushed the entrance of my pussy.

"Don't tease me."

"Oh, I'm not." His promise was soft and silky as he pushed into me. His cock stretched and filled me in a way that was mindblowing. Sucking my bottom lip, I closed my eyes as he steadily pressed fully inside me.

"Am I hurting you?" His hands drifted down my back and pulled at my hips.

"No." I pushed back against him, rocking my hips. "More."

His breathing quickened, and he sucked in air through his teeth. "Do that again."

I did as he requested as he started to move. Each time I pulled him inside me, I couldn't help but think that he belonged there, deep in my body. We were two parts of a beautiful union, the likes of which I'd never known. This was what mating felt like. I curled my fingers into the sheets, moaned with clenched teeth. I'd never had this with a man, and I knew that I would do all I could to keep him in my life for as long as he would allow it.

Shame pulled from me abruptly and stroked my back. "Lay on your back, I want to see your face when you come."

I turned on my knees to face him and met his gaze. Running one hand down his sweat-dampened chest to his stomach, I leaned forward and smiled when he moved closer. I moaned softly against his mouth and wrapped my arms around his neck. The kiss deepened, and his tongue thrust into my mouth.

He lifted me, coaxed my legs around his waist, and put me on my back. Breaking the kiss, he pressed his cock into me. I arched under him and shuddered when he slid his hands underneath and cupped my ass. The tips of my breasts hardened further against his chest, and all I could do was clutch at him.

Shame lifted his head and watched my face intently as he slowed his pace. The thick, nearly painful intrusion of his cock inside of me was suddenly more, and I shuddered underneath him with the power of it. He slid one hand between us and pressed his fingers against my clit. The rough stimulation, combined with the steady thrust of his body into mine, forced orgasm. I screamed with it, and he buried his face in the side of my neck as he came. His body jerked hard against me.

Several minutes passed, and then he slowly pulled his cock free. My pussy clenched against the sudden emptiness, and I took a deep breath. "That was awesome."

He laughed softly. "Yes, it was."

I sighed. "We gotta do that again."

"Soon." He turned his head and looked to me. "You're a beautiful woman."

"Thank you." I rolled on my side and propped up my head on one hand. "When you first saw me . . . what did you think?"

"That you looked like a goddess. A very cool and collected goddess. I also figured that I'd have to get pretty damn creative to get you in my studio."

"And your bed?"

"I'm rather arrogant. Seducing you seemed a lot easier than getting you to pose for me." He laughed when I frowned. "I really am very arrogant."

"Yes, you are." And I liked it. Arrogance had never been up there on my list of attractive qualities, but everything about Shamus Montgomery was attractive. I sat up reluctantly. "I should probably go home. I have an early morning."

He sat up and ran his fingers through my damp hair. "Stay with me. I want to wake up with you."

"Okay." Was it really this easy?

We were still for another moment, and then he sat up. "Shower?"

"Yes."

I rummaged around in my purse and pulled out a brush. I glanced back to the bed and leaned against the counter. Just looking at him made my mouth water. He rolled on to his side and met my gaze. I must have looked like a very hungry woman, because he smiled softly and sat up.

I ran the brush through my hair and watched him leave the bed.

"Are you about to use me for sex, Mercy?"

"Probably. How do you feel about it?"

He came to me, his gaze moving over my shoulders to my breasts. "You're putting me in a mood, Mercy."

"What kind of mood?"

"Possessive. Maybe a little rough." He ran his fingers gently across my jaw. "Are you up for that kind of play?

"I trust you," I murmured. "I would never confuse you with him."

"That's relieving to hear. Turn around."

I turned around and faced the mirror. Still, I watched his hands move over my shoulders and down my arms. He pressed me against his chest as his fingers trailed over my rib cage and then upward so that he could cup my breasts. Long, gentle fingers pulled at my nipples and twisted them gently as I arched my back.

I moved against his rapidly thickening cock and arched against his hands. "Shame."

He met my gaze in the mirror and then sank his teeth briefly into the spot where my shoulder and neck met. "Let me have you."

"Yes." I gasped softly and let my head fall back against his shoulder.

"Watch," he whispered and pressed me back against him as one hand slid downward to cover my pussy.

Fingers dipped into the folds of my sex and brushed against my aching clit. "Shame."

"Watch, Mercy."

I forced my eyes open and watched him in the mirror. His hands moved over me, his body moved against me, and his cock pressed against my ass and slid between my thighs. Placing my hands on the counter in front of me, I leaned forward. Shame murmured his approval and rolled my clit under his finger. I shuddered and closed my eyes briefly against the sharp pleasure.

"Don't close your eyes."

"It's too much." I bit down on my bottom lip and moaned when his fingers abandoned my clit. "Baby . . ."

"I'll give you what you need." He kissed my neck softly

and then pulled me further from the counter so that I could bend over more fully.

"The bed . . ."

He laughed softly. "Later."

I flushed and swallowed hard. "Okay."

I looked at his face in the mirror and saw his determination and need. It was hard to ignore how aroused he was. Every move he made brushed his hard cock against my thigh. Spreading my legs further, I whimpered as he slid one hand back down between my legs to play with my pussy. Two fingers slid into me, and I rocked back against the invasion until he removed his fingers abruptly.

He reached out past me on the counter and plucked up a box of condoms from a basket. I watched him free a condom and toss the bag aside. Remaining still while he rolled the latex into place took more effort than I'd ever thought possible. He pressed against the small of my back until I was bent into the position he wanted. I kept my gaze on his face, enthralled with the look of him.

The man had become the center of my world, and as he pushed his cock into me, I couldn't imagine a moment in my future without him. Hot, intense pleasure swept over me as he began to thrust deeply into my body. I pressed my hands against the counter and kept my gaze on him. Watching him push into my body again and again was just as arousing as the activity itself.

He lifted his eyes and looked in the mirror. Abruptly, he pulled from me and turned me around. I looped my arms around his neck as he lifted me off the floor and placed me on the counter.

Shame gripped my hips and thrust back into me. I pulled my legs up and wrapped them around his waist. Our gazes met as we began to rock against each other. The slick, sweet pain of his cock stretching and invading me took my breath with each thrust. I leaned back in his arms as he slipped a hand between us and slid two fingers between my labia to play with my clit.

"Fuck." I rocked against his fingers and cock with needy, jerky movements. I came in a hard rush of sensation, and tears streamed down my face.

"Yes." He buried his face in the side of the neck and then lifted me off the counter. "Hold on."

He walked to the bed and sat down. I clung to him while his hands slid down my back and cupped my ass. I slid up and down on him, as he seemed to want. Shame moaned softly against the side of my neck, and I shuddered at the power of the moment. I pushed him back on the bed and started to move faster.

"Mercy." Pleasure and frustration were laced in his voice as he said my name.

"Do you like this?"

"Yes." He gripped my hips and urged me on. "It's so good, baby."

I wanted to make him come. Shame continued to thrust upward against me, raising us both off the mattress completely time and time again. He pushed two fingers between us and into the wet folds of my pussy to press against my clit.

"Shame." I shuddered against his fingers and sat back on his thighs. "It's too much."

In a move that left me gasping, he turned us over and sank deep into me.

"Yes." I dragged my nails down his back and begged for more. "Fuck me."

"You're perfect," he gasped against my neck and thrust deep as he came.

CHAPTER 8

I had entered a sexual relationship with a man I barely knew, and I didn't feel an ounce of guilt or remorse. In fact, as I strolled into the gallery, displaying an incredible amount of afterglow, I couldn't even fake regret. I was so damn pleased with myself that the urge to tell everyone in the whole place that Shamus Montgomery had fucked me silly was overwhelming. Jane popped up from her desk the moment I finished coming up the stairs and followed along behind me into my office.

She closed the door and leaned on it. "Mercy, you got laid."

I laughed at the look of shock on her face and sat down in my chair. "I had a very productive weekend."

"I haven't seen a woman look that satisfied since I got my mother two pounds of Godiva chocolate for Mother's Day."

Momentarily distracted, I frowned at her. "You got your mom two pounds of Godiva for Mother's Day? I only got five pieces for Boss's Day."

Jane shrugged. "She pushed me out. You just sign my paycheck."

I laughed and nodded. "Well, it's good that you have priorities." I flipped open my calendar and looked over my schedule. Frowning, I looked at the appointment slated for late afternoon. "Jane, what is this at three?"

127

"Two gentlemen from the Met in New York are coming in to have a conference with you and Mr. Storey."

"Whatever for?" I demanded.

Jane stiffened, I imagine startled by my harsh tone. I couldn't help it.

She cleared her throat. "They're bringing an exhibit to Boston. We discussed this a month ago, Mercy."

"Yes, and only Edward was coming."

"He decided to bring a colleague along. I just added it to your calendar. I didn't think it would be a big deal. Dr. Morrison said he was looking forward to seeing you again and knew you would be pleased that he was bringing Mr. King with him. That you were all close friends when you worked there." She stopped talking, and I looked at her. She was staring at me hard. "You're pale, Mercy. What's wrong?"

I closed my eyes and turned in my chair to keep from giving the rest of the bull pen a show. I was shaking. My insides had tensed up so fast that I was starting to get a cramp in my side. Tears of frustration sprung in my eyes. It was infuriating that I couldn't control myself. Jane's silence was no blessing. There was no way I could tell her what I felt at that moment.

"Mercy, what have I done?" Jane asked softly.

How could I tell her that she'd invited a snake into our garden? I couldn't. I shook my head. "Nothing. I'm just not fond of Jeff King."

"It's too late to tell Dr. Morrison to come alone."

"I know." I blinked rapidly to keep the tears away. "When I move into Milton's office, I'm having fucking blinds put up in here and in there."

"That sounds like a good idea," Jane whispered.

"This just can't be happening," I finally said.

"I'm so sorry." Jane walked around so she could see my face. I knew from her expression that everything I was feeling was written all over my face.

"We'll attend the meeting, and under no circumstances are you to leave me alone with Jeff King." I wouldn't be a coward, but I wasn't going to give him an opportunity to hurt me again.

"I understand."

I looked at her, met her gaze, and realized that she did. "I'd like to be alone for a while. Would you call Dr. Price and ask her if I can have an hour this morning?"

Sitting at my desk, I tried to organize my thoughts about the coming meeting. I hadn't really thought about the meeting since I'd arranged it. I considered Edward Morrison a dear friend and had seen the meeting as something casual and unstructured. I'd talked him into letting the exhibit I had assembled for the museum come to Boston for a rare and brief appearance. It hadn't occurred to me that Jeff would find a way to come with Edward. It should have, and I felt like an idiot for the mistake.

The moment Lesley's assistant closed the door behind me, I sat down in the recliner and clutched my purse to my chest. It was like it happened yesterday. Like I'd never left New York. I took a deep breath and closed my eyes. Jeff King had taken over my world just by coming to Boston. I hated him for it. Actually, I hated him for a lot of reasons, but at the moment I hated him for being free to come to Boston.

"Normally I would let you sit there until you were ready to talk."

I opened my eyes and looked at her. She looked concerned, which surprised me. Lesley Price had always been very good at schooling her expression before. Even when the details of my rape had poured out of me in one explosive burst, she had sat in her chair with little emotion showing on her face.

"Jeff King is going to be in the gallery and in my office in two and half hours." I hated even saying it. But more than that, I hated the fear that saturated my voice. "I thought I was past this, but when I realized he'd been added to the meeting, my insides curled up. I feel ruined."

"It isn't uncommon for a woman to fear the presence of her abuser for years after the fact. You have every right to expect your world to be free of him. Unfortunately, since you chose not to prosecute him, that expectation is a little more difficult to make a reality. Is he still calling you?" She pressed her lips together in a thin line as if she wanted to say more.

"Yes." I nodded. "I've been getting hang-ups. I don't know for sure if those are him. However, the bastard did call me on my cell phone for a little chat. He asked me to meet with him. I refused and hung up on him."

"You said you feel ruined," Lesley reminded me softly.

"Like I did that night. When I was lying in my office where he'd left me. I couldn't get up, couldn't call for help." I pressed my fingers tightly to my lips to keep them from trembling. "I couldn't do anything but lie there, like he'd left me."

"But you didn't stay there. You got up, Mercy. You got up and you've built a life here in Boston that makes you happy."

"Yes."

"Jeff King can't take that away from you. He might try. He may see your success here as an offense. You were strong enough that you overcame what he did to you, and that might make him angry."

"I don't care what he thinks." I tried to relax and carefully put my purse down on the floor next the chair. "I can't care."

"Whether you like it or not, Mercy, this man made a lasting impression on your mind. The fact is that you might not ever have a day where you don't think about him. Shoving him and his actions into the back of your mind is not healthy."

"It works for me." I frowned. "No. That's a lie. It doesn't fucking work for me." I crossed my arms over my breasts and then glared at her. "I've been in therapy almost a year. I should be able to deal with this."

"I've been a Christian for forty-two years, and I can tell you with a great deal of certainty I'm not ready for the end of the world."

"And that means?" I demanded with a frown.

"It means, Mercy, that you can prepare for something your whole life, and it can still leave you lying flat on your back, wondering what the hell happened. Life is not predictable, and trying to control it will only drive you insane."

"And I should take each day as it comes." She'd told me that a time or two. It wasn't a piece of advice I had ever taken to heart. "I went to bed with Shamus last night."

"Good." She leaned back in her chair and watched me sit down. "Were there any moments of fear or regret?"

"No, none. I'm very comfortable and secure with him." I relaxed a little, relieved that she'd accepted my abrupt change of subject.

"Do you think you rushed this?"

"I want to say yes, because it seems like the thing to say." Shrugging, I sighed and then chuckled. "It's like when I was a kid and I did something bad that I really enjoyed, and my mother would force me to apologize. I would do it, but I never meant it."

"Does it help to think about him?"

"Yes." I nodded.

"But it doesn't push Jeff King away completely."

"No. I'm not sure what to do today. I want to scream at him and take from him until he feels as badly as I do. What do I do?"

Lesley stood up from her desk and walked around to stand in front of it. She leaned on the desk and was silent for a moment. Finally she said, "Under no circumstances are you to agree to meet this man outside of the professional arena. You make it clear that you consider any contact on his part to be harassment, and be prepared to involve the police if he doesn't pay attention. Even without a rape conviction, antistalking laws will protect you on this front. Be strong, be firm, and do not give him the opportunity to get under your skin.

"This is easy for me to say, I suppose, but a man like Jeff King gets his kicks from power. He wants your fear, and needs to believe that he ruined you in New York. Once he realizes that you aren't a shattered and devastated victim, he could become a serious threat. Do not underestimate him, and make your stand in a place where help is available to you."

I nodded and sighed. "Be strong, don't take his shit, and call the police if he doesn't get the hint."

Lesley laughed. "Yes, basically."

"And if I can't? I couldn't make myself call the police when he raped me."

"You can. He's not in charge of your life, and he can't control you. Jeff King is nothing. He's a worthless man who needs to brutalize women to feel empowered."

Jane was at her desk when I came in the door. One glance at my office told me why she looked so defeated. They were early. I walked to Jane's desk and picked up my messages.

"I'm so freaking sorry, Mercy."

The guilt written all over her face made me feel small and furious. I would've never wanted to upset her so. Her friendship was more important than I'd allowed myself to admit. "No worries, Jane. Did you offer them coffee?"

"Yes, they both declined. I'll have the conference room ready in a few minutes. If you want, we can start the meeting early."

I looked at my watch and raised an eyebrow. "I didn't realize I'd been gone so long. Let me know when Milton is ready and the conference room is set up. Remind me, what did we offer them for the collection?"

"Central floor, second level."

Edward met me at the door of my office with his hands outstretched and a genuine smile of affection. I'd missed him. He was one of the best men I'd ever met. He loved his wife and his children as if they were the only things that mattered. I liked that about him; his loyalty and devotion were endearing. Accepting his embrace, I glanced briefly at Jeff, who had stood as well.

"Jeff."

"Mercy." I hated my name on his lips, and I wanted to beat his face in so that he could never say it again.

I went to my desk and took a seat. Dropping my purse in the drawer next to me, I directed my gaze to Edward. "I have my assistant setting up our conference space. As soon as Mr. Storey is free, we can begin."

Edward smiled. "See, Jeff, I told you our Mercy would have things well in hand here."

I looked at Jeff and found him staring at me. His expression was a mixture of confusion and anger. "Jeff has always underestimated me." I looked at Jane, who gave me a nod. "We can move into the conference room now. Edward, I'm sure you'll find the space ideal for the Impressionist exhibit. I'm surprised, however, that you are letting it travel."

"I can't hold all the beautiful things at once." Edward smiled. "It wouldn't be fair."

"I have some slides of shows we've done before in the central area. It'll give you an idea of what we can do." I entered the conference room ahead of them, but waited until they'd both chosen chairs before I sat down a few chairs from Jane.

She looked professional but wound so tight I was surprised her skin wasn't stretching. I regretted letting her see my anxiety. Milton hurried in and filled up the silence with his chatter, and then I began the slide show. I have no idea what I said or even if the presentation went well. Each time my gaze fell on Jeff, my insides twisted up. By the time I sat down and Jane turned the lights back on, I felt like I'd run a marathon.

As soon as my presentation was over, I left the conference room and left the details to Milton and Jane. I couldn't take another moment of it. Once in my office I turned on my radio, sat behind my desk, and stared at the wall in front of me. I'd been staring at the wall for nearly twenty minutes when my office door opened. I looked up to speak to Jane, but it wasn't her.

"What do you want, Jeff?" I asked in disbelief.

"I thought we could have dinner together." Jeff leaned against the door frame as if he hadn't a care in the world.

I felt like a cartoon character, my mouth hanging open in shock. I clamped it shut so hard that my teeth snapped. My fingers grabbed the armrest of my chair. "Are you out of your fucking mind?"

"We were friends once."

"I thought so, and then you raped me. You were a twisted presence in my life, and I'm fortunate to have survived you. Now you're nothing to me."

The silence fell like a rock between us. Jeff was one of those men who never accepted responsibility for his actions, and a part of me deeply regretted not making him pay for what he'd done to me. He pulled my office door shut and paced in front of it as if he had something to work out. I couldn't imagine that he had anything to say that would make me think less of him, but then I was never good at judging him.

"It was a mistake."

"A mistake?" I demanded, nearly overwhelmed by the statement. "Rape is a crime, not a mistake. Get out of my office."

"Mercy, we can fix this between us."

"Every time I look at you, I can hear myself begging you to

stop." I sucked in a breath. "And you didn't. You violated me, and there is nothing that can be said that will change that."

The muscle in his jaw worked as he looked at me. "I'm asking you to forgive me."

"Leave."

"Mercy."

"Get out, and don't ever come back. You aren't welcome in Holman's, professionally or otherwise. When the Impressionist exhibit comes here this winter, you will remain in New York."

"It's my exhibit."

"I don't care." And it was *my* exhibit. He'd taken it over only because I had left it behind.

"Edward will expect me to come with him for the initial setup."

"If you come with him, Jeff, I'll tell him what you did to me. I'll tell him the real reason why I left the museum and New York. Just how much do you think he'll value you after that?"

He flushed, red and angry. "That would ruin my career."

"It would be no less than you deserve. You tried to ruin my soul." I stood, unwilling to sit. "Get out." I looked past him, to Jane, who was standing just outside the door. "Get out, or I'll have my assistant call security to escort you out."

When he was gone from my sight, I went to the bathroom off my office and shut the door. I could only be grateful the idiot who had designed our office space hadn't made the bathroom walls out of glass, too. Dropping the lid down on the toilet, I sat down. When Jane peeked in, I frowned at her.

"I didn't think I would have to endure people coming into the bathroom with me until I had children."

Jane closed the door and leaned on it. "What did Jeff King do to you, Mercy?"

"This isn't a conversation that a supervisor and subordinate should have," I finally said.

"Fine, then tell me because I'm your friend."

I let my gaze travel back to her face, and knew she didn't want to know. "I'm sorry, Jane. None of this is your fault, and I'm sorry that I've upset you so."

"Did you have an affair with him?"

"No." I stood from the toilet and frowned. It was weird being in the bathroom with Jane. I laughed then, struck by the absurdity of it.

Jane frowned at me as she opened the door. I followed her out, knowing that she wasn't going to give up. She sat down in a chair in front of my desk as I walked to the windows. The parking lot was half empty. "We should try to find a way to bring people into the gallery on their lunch hours."

Jane snorted. "Not unless we want to set up food sample carts for them to graze on while they browse."

I looked back to her. "He forced me to have sex with him."

The word hovered on her lips as the color slipped rapidly from her face. Anger and a look only another woman understands flashed in her eyes. She stood and shoved her hands into her pockets. She looked so young and vulnerable then. Jane was two years younger than I was, but I felt so much older. She cleared her throat and shook her head.

"It's all right, Jane. No one knows what to say after such a confession, and when they do speak, they inevitably screw it up so badly they feel worse. I'll be fine."

"I'll make sure security understands that he's not to come back in the building." She walked towards the door.

"What will you tell them?"

"I'll tell them he grabbed my ass." Jane smiled then, but her eyes remained dark and angry. "Mr. Wilkes can't stand a man with no manners. He won't get past the door without me being notified."

I said nothing else, and she left my office.

* * *

I sat outside Shame's gallery, confused and angry that the decision to come to him had been so natural. What a fool I was, slipping into a man's life and bed without a single thought to my emotional safety.

Deep down inside, I knew that he would never hurt me physically. It was as if I'd developed a sixth sense about men since I had been attacked. I had met a man here or there that I hadn't trusted, who had set me on edge the moment I met them. Shamus Montgomery, artist and fuck of the century, didn't make me want to run for my life.

I got out of my car, angry with myself for falling into a relationship where I was emotionally and physically needy. It didn't take a rocket scientist to tell me that I didn't want Shame to be the needy one. I needed him to be strong and re-silient. I had to know that he was there, full of life and pas-sion. That he was ready and able to fill me with his strength and, of course, his cock.

Entering the gallery, I pulled the key from the door as I locked it and hurried up the steps. I stopped at the top of the stairs, stunned and furious. As women went, she was an ex-ceptional one, tall and sleek in a way that runway models were. Her dark skin looked oiled, and I fleetingly wondered if she'd applied the oil herself. I took the final step and a deep calming breath. I would just have to get used to the fact that Shame worked with naked women. The alabaster was cov-ered, and he was working on a bronze project I'd seen only once. It had been covered the other times I'd been there.

The woman hadn't looked at me, though I knew she was aware of my presence. She'd stiffened, but kept her pose. I would have never agreed to such a pose. She was kneeling on the platform, her arms over her head, back arched. It looked uncomfortable as hell. I walked toward the stairs that led to Shame's private space, and I heard an audible intake of breath.

I looked over my shoulder and raised one eyebrow at her before I went up the stairs.

By the time I'd found a bottle of wine, a corkscrew, and a glass, Shame was walking up the stairs. I poured a generous portion and took the bottle with me as I headed toward the couches where his big television was located. I admit, I have no idea why men insist on having such big televisions. However, his flat-panel was fascinating. I'd never watched a flat-panel television, except at the store.

He followed me to the couch with an empty glass and sat down beside me as he grabbed the bottle. "You just cost me a model."

"Excuse me?" I raised an eyebrow.

He sighed and took a deep swallow of his wine. "She apparently had some personal ambitions that I was unaware of."

"Oh, you poor brilliant artist. How trying it must be when young, naked, nubile women throw themselves at you all the time."

Shame stared at me for a moment and then started to laugh. "Well, I guess that is an odd thing for a man to complain about."

"Indeed." I pointed toward the television. "Turn that thing on, and I want the remote."

"I take it I'm not getting you naked tonight."

"Oh, you can get me naked, but I'm not sitting in that chair tonight." I took the remote after he turned the television on and looked over the buttons. I started flipping.

The best thing about flipping channels is being the flipper. There is a fine art to flipping channels, an art lost on most men who rarely pause on anything besides naked women and sporting events. Also, as the flipper, the rapidly changing picture isn't annoying. The person actually in control of the flipping enjoys it.

"If you don't find something to watch soon, I'm going to call my cable company and report you for abuse."

"Go ahead." I took another sip of wine. "If they don't like it, they can fuck off."

"I never thought I'd say this, but you're kind of sexy when you are in a bad mood."

"I'm well past being in a bad mood."

"I am a very fortunate man." He took a deep swallow of wine and sighed when I stopped the television on a channel with a documentary on it.

I said, "I've often wondered if dinosaurs really looked like we think. I mean, sure we can get the bones together. But, hell, for all we know, some of them could have been purple."

He laughed. "I'm sure there are people who get paid a great deal of money to think about things like that."

"Sometimes I think I'd like a simple job. Maybe I'd like to be that person who sits by the Emergency Alert System button. I mean, seriously, beyond the tests, has that thing actually ever been used? I don't think so."

"I doubt somebody is sitting beside it."

"Don't ruin my stress-free fantasy. If you can't contribute to it, just be quiet." I looked from my empty glass to the bottle and frowned. I really didn't need another glass.

"Are you going to tell what's wrong?"

"I had a meeting today with Edward Morrison; it had been planned for some time. However, he called a few weeks ago and added Jeff King to the meeting, and Jane didn't tell me. I found out this morning. He showed up, we had a meeting, he asked me to have dinner with him, and I told him no."

"Why didn't you tell me?" he asked softly, his voice full surprise and anger.

"What? Was I supposed to come running to you with my problem?" I demanded, and then flushed at the harsh tone

139

I'd used. "It was less stressful than I'd thought it would be, and a great deal more painful." I cleared my throat.

I watched him pour more wine into my glass, and I met his gaze. His face, beautiful and angelic, was a picture of anger. Watching him fight past his own anger was an interesting experience. Jealous of the control he had, I turned away from him and shrugged.

"The fact that you had to be in the same room with that bastard makes me sick."

"It's my own fault. Had I pressed charges, even if he'd gone free . . ." I sighed. "Even if he'd been found not guilty of assaulting me, I doubt Edward would have brought him to Boston for today's meeting."

"Did you tell Edward what happened to you?"

"No. He knew that Jeff and I didn't part on good terms, but I think he assumed it was professional. Two months before it happened, I was promoted above him. It wasn't a secret that Jeff resented it. It hardly mattered that I had more experience and education."

"He resented you."

"At first his comments seemed like good-natured teasing. But when others would've let it go, he continued. It never occurred to me that . . . he would be violent."

"Until he raped you."

"Yes." I swallowed hard. I hated hearing Shame say it.

Shame spoke again. "I'd like to think that I could make this all right for you. I want to believe that I can make you forget the man ever existed, but I know that's not within my abilities. I hate him for touching you in a way that cannot be wiped away or forgotten."

His words were tight and controlled. I could see the frustration and anger in him.

"I know."

"Are you hungry?" he asked.

"No." I set my wine down. "Will you take me to bed?"

"Are you sure that's what you want right now?"

"It's what I need."

He stood and pulled me from the couch. I followed him up the stairs, slipping my hands into the back pockets of his jeans. He turned to me and brought me close as we stopped by the bed. His eyes were dark and intent on my face as he pulled my blouse from the waistband of my skirt and then unbuttoned it. He pushed the silk off my shoulders, and I let it fall to the floor.

His fingers brushed along the shoulder straps of my bra, then slipped around to unfasten it. The clasp gave away easily to his fingers, and I let the bra drop to the floor. Placing a series of soft and delicate kisses along my neck, he unzipped my skirt and pushed it carefully past my hips. It was like being undressed by soft invisible hands. So gentle and careful, it made my breath catch in my throat.

I stepped out of the puddle my skirt made and pushed the material out of the way. "Shame."

"Yes, Mercy?"

"What are you doing?" I asked softly, as he knelt on his knees and placed a soft kiss on my stomach.

"Undressing you."

I held onto his shoulders as he unfastened my sandals and removed them one at a time from my feet. Soft whispering fingers moved along my thighs, and he slipped his fingers along the edges of my panties before gently tugging on them and drawing them down my legs. I took a deep breath as I stepped out of them. Shame had reduced me to a mindless girl just by undressing me. My body was burning, my stomach was clenched, and my nipples were so hard it was nearly an agony not to have his hands on them.

I lay down on the bed as he pulled his shirt off and unzipped his jeans. Once he was free of the jeans and boxers, I could see that undressing me had aroused him as well. His cock jutted thick and hard out from his body. Boy, did I love his cock. Did I love him? I didn't know if I'd crossed that line, but it felt like a sure thing. This man filled me in many ways.

He put one knee on the bed and then the other. I watched him, his gaze moving over the length of my body and pausing on my clean-shaven pussy. I hadn't shaved for a man in years. I'd been so surprised that it had even occurred to me. His fingers brushed over my bare labia and then gently between them before he lowered his head and nuzzled his mouth against that warm, moist flesh.

I spread my legs and ran my hands over his head as his mouth sank into me. Hell yes, I thought, there was nothing like a man who had a big dick and could eat pussy like a starving man. I moved under his mouth, and his tongue alternately dipped into me and whipped up to tease at my clit. Two blunt fingers pushed into me, and I cried out from the pleasure of it.

He lifted his head and I met his gaze. His fingers were pushing deep in me, and he watched my body respond, his gaze sweeping over my hips that I couldn't keep still, to the hands I had clasped on my breasts, then to my mouth. He moved his fingers then and used his thumb to tease my clit. I groaned softly and closed my eyes.

"No, don't close your eyes."

I opened them again, though it was hard, and met his gaze. I would give him anything he wanted, and we both knew it. I sucked my bottom lip again and jerked against his hand. God, it was killing me—the hot and sweet pleasure of his fingers was astounding and thoroughly painful. It was that sharp, devastating sort of pain that comes when the pleasure is too much and the lust intensifies to a point that makes your insides boil.

"Don't hold back," he whispered. "Tell me how much you like it."

I released my lip and ran my tongue over the swollen flesh. "God, Shame, you're killing me."

He laughed and glanced toward the nightstand. "Stay right here."

I arched as he pulled his fingers from me and left the bed for a condom. I couldn't stay still. Rolling to my knees, I crawled to where he stood beside the bed and reached for him. I pulled the condom from his hand and brought him around so I could slip his cock into my mouth. He was big enough that it was difficult to get the head of him in. Running my hands along the length of him, I licked and sucked as much of him as I could get into my mouth until he jerked against me and carefully pulled his cock away.

When I looked up to his face, I knew he'd felt what I felt. I tore open the condom and pulled the latex free. Rolling it into place with my hand, I squeezed my legs together. My pussy was alternately tightening and relaxing. My body knew what was coming, and it was more than ready to take every inch he had to offer.

Lying back on the bed, I spread my legs and held my hand out for him. He moved to kneel on the bed, scooted closer, and lifted my hips as he pressed the head of his cock into me. Hot and stinging, the penetration of his cock was exactly what I needed. My body stretched and then consumed him as I wrapped my legs around his waist.

He kissed my mouth gently as he let me take some of his weight. "Did you shave for me?"

"Yes."

"Good."

"I shouldn't care what you think," I admitted as he began to thrust in and out of me. The careful stroke of his body was making me feel bereft and victorious at the same time. The combination was startling and so satisfying.

I arched under him, took the deep thrust of his cock in one shuddering breath. "Yes."

"Will you take more?" he asked softly and slid his hands up under my ass. He tilted my hips and sank more deeply into me.

"Fuck." I clutched at his back and took in a deep breath. "Baby, please."

"Say it." He stilled and our gazes locked in the dimly lit room.

My hands loosened on his back and slipped in the dampness I found there. "I want everything you have."

And I did. I wanted him in every way possible, and I wondered fleetingly how he'd come to mean so much in so short a time. I wrapped myself around Shame and held on tightly as he pushed his cock in and out of my body. The blending of flesh had never felt more primitive or more right. I rushed wet against his invasion and cried out with the pleasure of it.

CHAPTER 9

I'd spent the night with Shame, which had meant that I'd made a mad dash across town to my apartment to shower and change for work. I was twenty minutes late for work, which was unusual for me. I walked into the gallery and toward the stairs that led to the private offices without a single glance around the floor. As expected, Jane was at her desk. She offered me a tight smile as she stood, grabbed several folders, and prepared to follow me into my office.

My agenda for the day was full, and I didn't expect a break until after Milton's contract expired. He mucked the works up at every opportunity, and the Board would have fired him if it hadn't been for the generous severance-package clause in his contract. He might be a little troll, but he had his bright moments. Therefore, until he was gone I was left to produce the things the Board expected from me, while not thoroughly burning my bridges with Milton. Milton had his circle of friends, and since some of them spent obscene amounts of money in the gallery, I couldn't afford to alienate him completely.

"What's first?" I asked Jane.

"An unmitigated disaster."

I glanced toward Jane, alarmed. "Such big words before lunch, what's going on?"

She bit down on her lip and sat down in the chair she favored. Crossing her legs, she looked at me with a straight face. "Lisa Millhouse had Sarah arrested for trespassing yesterday afternoon."

I blew air through my lips as I struggled to keep a straight face. "Did she make bail?"

Jane looked out the window and seemed to be chewing the inside of her cheek. She cleared her throat. "Yes. The charges were dropped, but a restraining order was filed."

"Oh. My. God." I looked at the ceiling and then let my gaze move out to the bullpen. Sarah's desk was empty and cleared. "She quit?"

Jane sighed. "Yes. She threw a genuine conniption fit and packed up all of her stuff."

"Conniption fit?" I asked softly.

"Yes, that's more than a hissy fit, but less than a psychotic episode."

"I love it when you get all southern."

Jane laughed and shrugged. I knew she'd spent several years shedding her accent, and had pretty much washed the country right out of her. It was a shame, but I knew why. A woman had a difficult enough time in the art world anyway, without adding "southern" to the mix. Unfair or not, there were a few people out there who thought that southern equaled stupid, or at the very least, so unsophisticated that they wouldn't be capable of functioning in the art world.

"Where's Milton?"

"He's on the phone with James Brooks insisting the gallery sever our relationship with Lisa. To quote him, 'She's an uncivilized harridan.'"

I glanced to my phone and, after a moment, I sighed. "What more could go wrong today?"

"I'm saving the worst news for last."

I focused on her, aware that she was now serious. "Okay."

"He's still here."

I didn't have to ask who. "I see."

"He has a meeting with Mr. Storey at ten this morning. I heard from Mr. Storey's secretary that Storey is going to offer King a job."

"As what?"

"Storey called a Board meeting. He's going to suggest that Jeff King take his place."

"He knows that is my job," I snapped.

"Storey has told the board that you're responsible for the situation with Lisa Millhouse and Sarah's arrest. He's drafted a report suggesting that you assigned her to Lisa's account to get rid of her, and that you conspired with an artist to discredit him."

"If I'd assigned Sarah to the account, how is it that I discredited him?" I asked softly, my temper almost at the boiling point.

"I have no idea."

Jane was slumping in the chair when I finally looked at her. I pushed my hair off my shoulders and pulled it up in my hands to keep them busy. After a while, I released my hair and dropped my hands to my lap. "Is Jeff here yet?"

"Yes, security escorted him to the small conference room." She smirked as she said it.

Her pleasure at squeezing Jeff amused me, but I didn't have enough energy to laugh. Yesterday had been hard, but I'd been able to hold on to the fact that he would be gone again soon. Yet Milton had invited him back into my haven. I suppose because he'd noticed how tense I'd been with Jeff during the meeting. "Milton is such a jackass."

"Yes."

"I won't run from them, either one of the bastards. When is James due to arrive?"

"Mr. Brooks e-mailed me and asked me to make sure you were in the meeting. You have about a half hour to prepare."

I stood from my chair. "Okay, let me be alone for a while."

I didn't look back, but I heard the door shut gently. Jane

was a unique person, brash and bold when it was least expected, and so damn gracious and soft the next moment. I valued her as my friend long before I had even realized she was my friend.

When I had awakened this morning, wrapped in Shame's arms, I'd felt safe and content. The drama of the situation in front of me was almost laughable. My troll boss was trying to maneuver a man who had raped me into a position of authority over me. Yet I couldn't laugh; not a single part of me felt like laughing. Knowing that Jeff was in the same building with me was sucking the life out of me.

I jerked as the door to my office opened, and turned to the sound. I thought fleetingly about getting the hinges oiled, again, as Shamus walked purposefully across the room to me. "Hey."

He looked around the room. "Mercy, you have a glass wall."

I laughed and shrugged. "It is a pain. It's like working in a fishbowl."

Shame sighed and looked around to the bull pen—fourteen pairs of eyes were looking right back. He sighed. "There goes my plan to do something perfectly filthy to you in your office."

"I could fire them all and close the gallery." He laughed and he pulled me into his arms for a hug. I accepted his embrace and sighed into the skin of his neck. "How did you know I needed to see you?"

"I didn't." He touched my face carefully and ran his hand down my neck. "I needed to see you. What's wrong?"

"The situation with Milton has come to a head. I have a meeting in about thirty minutes with him, the Board, and Jeff King."

"King's here?"

"Yes." I looked at his face and didn't find the anger I expected. He looked so calm, and so very ready to be the center of my world. I didn't know what I'd done in my life to deserve him.

"Why is he here?"

"That asshole, Milton, is going to suggest him as the new director."

"Why?"

"To thwart me." I glanced at Jane, who was trying hard not to stare with the rest of the audience. I laughed softly. "He's such an ass, but unfortunately Jeff is qualified for the position."

"Will James Brooks agree to this just to get rid of Storey?"

"I don't know." I hated the admission, but suddenly the place I'd built with the gallery didn't seem stable. James Brooks would do a lot at this point to get rid of Milton, and I wasn't sure if that included shafting me.

"If I kissed you right now, it would probably look bad."

My gaze lingered on his mouth as I nodded. "Yes, I suppose it would."

"That's such a shame." He took a step back from me and then walked to sit in one of the chairs in front of my desk. "I want to stay while you are in the meeting."

My knee-jerk reaction was to tell him no, but I paused and allowed myself a moment to think. Shamus Montgomery was one big, gorgeous reminder of what I could do for the gallery. However, all I could really think was that after the meeting was over, I could crawl into Shame and forget about all of them.

I sat down in my chair as the door to my office opened under the hand of James Brooks. He was a formidable man. When I'd first met him, I'd felt about two feet tall. Standing next to him was still rather ego deflating. I didn't know what about him did that to me and nearly everyone else I knew, but there it was.

"James." I said his name as sort of a plea, and that threw me off balance.

"Mercy." He looked at Shame and offered his hand. "Shamus, it's good to see you here. I was pleased when Mercy signed you."

Shame stood and took his hand. "So was I." Shame looked out into the bull pen. "Mercy was telling me that Storey has found someone he would support as his replacement."

"Yes, that is the message I received." James sat down, slouched in much the same way Shame did, and looked at me. "Give me one good reason why Jeff King can't be here."

The words fell out of my mouth so hard and unrelenting that both men flinched. "He's a waste of flesh and bone. If the Board were to accept Milton's recommendation, I would quit and sue you for breach of contract. I signed my contract with the understanding that I would be made director."

James cleared his throat and glanced briefly at Shame, who was staring at the floor. "I see. As always, Mercy, you make your point clearly and precisely."

"I try."

He looked at me then and, to my amazement, laughed. He rubbed his face and then said, "Well, come on then. If I'm going to suffer that ass for the second time in a week, I'm not doing it alone. Want to come along, Shamus?"

Startled, I glanced between the two men and cleared my throat. "I think Mr. Montgomery would be more comfortable waiting here."

James looked at me briefly and then shook his head. "Come along, Shamus. You'll enjoy watching Storey preen like a peacock. He's rather good at it. If I were hunting man, I'd shoot him and mount him on my wall."

I followed along behind the two of them and glared pointedly at Jane until she hopped up and followed me. If I was going to be involved in this testosterone festival, I wanted backup. Once in the conference room, I sat on the far end, away from all of the men in the room. Only Brooks was on hand from the Board, and since he owned the gallery, he was enough.

"I wasn't aware that Ms. Rothell was going to be attending this meeting," Milton snapped.

Jane flipped open her notebook and clicked her pen smartly. "Should I write that down?"

"Yes." I inclined my head. "I was invited, Milton. So why don't you just get started?"

He cleared his throat. "As it may be known, I plan to retire in August."

Jane snorted, and I looked at her with what I hoped was look of censure. It was hard since I'd had to bite my tongue to keep from laughing. We both returned our attention to Milton, who had stopped to glare at us. I cleared my throat and raised an eyebrow.

"I've interviewed Dr. Jeff King and believe he would be an asset to the gallery. His education is above reproach, and he has an eye for beauty." Milton looked toward Brooks. "I'd like to place Jeff in my role here at the gallery and train him to take my place when I leave in August."

James looked at Jeff briefly and then focused on Milton. "As you well know, I will not place the Holman Gallery in the hands of an individual I don't know or trust. I chose Mercy Rothell to take your place, and in August she will."

Jeff straightened in his chair. "I understand. However, I am interested in a position here. With Ms. Rothell moving into the director's place, her position will be available."

James glanced at me and shook his head. "Mercy will choose the person that goes into the Assistant Director position. She's in the best place to make such a choice."

Score two for the home team. I stood from my chair and smoothed my skirt. I said, "I believe we are done here."

I shoved my apartment door open with one hip and dumped two bags of groceries on the obscenely expensive table I'd bought for the entranceway. I pulled the door shut and locked it with a twist of my wrist. I was so ready for some alone time. I'd spent an hour with Shamus while he worked and then, after a long and thorough kiss, he'd sent me home.

It irked that he understood me well enough to know that I needed the space. I felt I barely knew him at all. I took the groceries to the kitchen and started to put them away, which, of course, meant that everything that was perishable went in the refrigerator and the rest was left on the counter.

Pouring myself a generous glass of wine, I went into the living room and pushed the button on my answering machine. Two hang-ups, an automated phone survey company, and then silence. I looked at the answering machine and jumped when Jeff King's voice filled the space of my home.

"You've always been in my way, Mercy. First at the museum, prancing around that place and holding court with anyone that could get you further in life. You fucked your way up the ladder there, and you're doing the same thing at Holman's. I saw the way Brooks looked at you. I know what you are and how far you'll go to get what you don't fucking deserve."

Disgusted with his verbal abuse, I turned off the machine. I went to my front door, locked all four locks, and put the chain in place. Back in the living room, I sat down on the couch. I'd drained half the glass when the phone rang. I wasn't going to be a coward, so I picked it up.

"Hello."

"Hey, I'm regretting sending you home."

I sighed and stood. "Shamus." Going to a window, I peeked out into the night and knew that I didn't want to spend it alone. "Why don't you come over here and spend the night in my bed?"

"That sounds perfect; I'll be there in about thirty minutes."

After I hung up, I went into the kitchen and put up the rest of the groceries. I let myself think about Jeff and the situation that had developed during the day. I couldn't have imagined anything worse if I had tried. Beyond the drama of it all, I felt like I'd fallen into some awkward and warped universe where everything good and bad happened at once.

I had a man in my life again, a sexy and thoughtful man who looked at me as if I were special. Being special for him meant so much to me, I hated that my past was bleeding onto us. I picked up my phone and dialed Lisa Millhouse's number. I'd meant to call her earlier in the day, but had forgotten.

"Hello, there, I expected to hear from you sooner."

I leaned against the counter and put my wineglass down. "Where should I start?"

"The woman wanted me to do a fucking television interview! She invited a crew out here to my home!"

I sighed. "Did you get them all with the paint gun?"

Lisa laughed softly. "No, I wouldn't want that sort of behavior on tape. I just called the police and reported them as trespassers." She was silent for a minute, and then softly she asked, "What's wrong, Mercy?"

"Whenever I think that I'm on the right path, that I've found a good stride, something fucks me up."

"I could be flippant and say that's life." She stopped and then sighed. "But it doesn't make you feel better. I've heard that a well-placed cock can cure what ails you."

I snorted. "You've been talking to Jane."

"She offers sound advice," Lisa laughed. "However, the poor girl doesn't even own a vibrator. I can't believe you let her out in the world without one."

"She insists that she doesn't need one."

"Yeah, and I don't need oxygen," Lisa returned.

I closed my eyes and nodded. "Thanks."

"I'm sure one day you'll return the favor."

"When you are ready to tell me more about what happened, I'll be available."

"I know."

"Shame is on his way over here."

"Good for you." Lisa yawned. "Fuck him for me, too."

I laughed and wondered why it didn't bother me that she'd had a relationship with him. "I just might. Would you like him to call me your name?"

Lisa laughed aloud. "What a freaky lady you are, Mercy. I don't think Shame stands a chance. Have fun."

I told her good night and turned off the phone. I put it down on the counter and picked up my wineglass as the doorbell rang. I went to it, focused on Shamus and all the warm, wonderful feelings he stirred in me. Unlocking the door, I peeked out the peephole and jerked back from the door. Swallowing hard, I put my wineglass carefully down on the table. Only the chain remained in place.

That shiny gold-plated chain was the only thing between Jeff King and me. With a shaking hand, I reached toward the door. My fingers grazed the first bolt lock as the door pushed open and slammed against the chain. I screamed before I could help myself and ran toward the kitchen for my phone.

I ran past the phone in a wild moment that I can only describe as desperate and stupid. I heard the chain give away as I threw open my bedroom closet and pulled out my baseball bat. The steel bat felt good in my hands, though I wished I'd had the guts to buy a gun. Turning toward the doorway, I waited for Jeff to make his way to the bedroom.

He came to the doorway of the bedroom, and his hand moved up the wall, searching for the light switch. The light flipped on, and there he stood. Fear and hatred that made me feel small and wounded boiled inside me as he just stood there and looked at me. "You and I need to talk."

"No, we don't."

He glanced briefly at the bat, and a smile briefly crossed his lips. "Do you think for a moment that moving here was an escape for you? I've known where you were all along. You don't need to pretend anymore. No need to be outraged when we both know you enjoyed it."

I swallowed back bile and gripped the bat a little bit tighter. "Get the hell out of my life."

"You don't have the right to deny me. You are nothing."

"Your delusions don't make what you did to me right. You're a sick bastard who can't get off without some illusion of domination. You didn't break me, didn't beat me. I'm stronger for what you did to me, not weaker. You'll never win."

He came at me, and I honestly don't think he expected me to swing. But I did. I swung with all of the strength I had. He fell to his knees, and I struck him hard across the back. He fell on the floor, and I just stood there, like a ninny, staring at him. If I had been watching this on television, I would have been screaming at the woman to run while she had the chance.

Understanding why I wasn't running, I lowered the bat until it pointed at the floor. I wanted to beat him bloody.

I jumped when I heard my name. Then I called back, "Shame?"

He appeared in the doorway several seconds later and looked from Jeff to me. "This is not exactly what I had in mind."

I shrugged and lowered the bat. "He broke the chain on my door."

"I noticed." Shame kicked him, and Jeff groaned. "Hey, asshole, you want to get up so I can kill you?"

"I'm handling this." I pointed one finger at him and then looked at Jeff. "Get out of my apartment."

"You aren't going to call the police?"

"No." From Shame's shocked expression, I realized that he fully expected me to call the police and have Jeff arrested for breaking into my apartment. I knew I wouldn't. How could I? The man had raped me, and I hadn't filed charges against him . . . and explaining that to yet another cop wasn't something I could imagine myself doing.

Jeff got to his knees and cast Shamus a leery glance. The hostility radiating off them both practically glowed. I could imagine that Jeff was pretty pissed that I'd beat him up. He was one of those men who held his masculinity near and dear to his heart.

On his feet, he rubbed his mouth and kept looking from me to Shame. "You're fucking this guy?"

"Jeff, you should leave before he decides that he'd like to hurt you more than he'd like to keep seeing me." I tightened my grip on the bat and stilled the urge to hit him again.

Jeff walked toward Shame, and when he didn't step aside to let him leave, Jeff swung. To Shame's credit, he let the punch land before he struck back. Then Jeff was, once more, lying on the floor between us, bleeding from the nose and mouth. I watched the blood gush to the surface, amazed.

"Leave, Jeff, or I swear to God I'll call the cops and tell them that I beat an intruder to death."

Both men looked toward me in shock.

Swallowing hard, I tried to remember that I was the civilized one.

Stepping over Jeff, I left the bedroom and went into the hall bathroom, shut the door, and locked it. Thankful that I had taken the time to clean my bathroom, I sank to my knees. My insides were shaking with anger and fear. I hated the fear, the weakness of it. Hadn't I stood up to him? Nausea threatened, but giving into that would have been horrifying. Sitting there on the floor, I fought the urge to rock. Where had my courage and resolve disappeared to?

A few minutes passed before I heard scuffling in the hallway and assumed that Shame was taking Jeff out of the building. I stood when someone knocked on the bathroom door.

"What?"

It was Shame. "Mercy, I don't appreciate being on the other side of a locked door."

I went to the door and unlocked it.

He opened the door and looked at me. "Are you okay?"

I shrugged and propped my bat against the bathroom counter. "Did you hurt him?"

"I put him in a cab."

"That's not what I asked."

"I know."

"Damn it, Shame!"

"You don't get to be mad at me, Mercy." He pointed a finger at me. "What the hell were you thinking, unlocking your door without looking to see who was on the other side?"

"Don't you yell at me! I'm a grown woman, and I don't need to be lectured!" And I stomped my foot to make my point.

He looked me over and then reached out for me. I went angry but willing. He pulled me tight to him and ran one hand through my hair. "You kicked his ass."

"I did," I whispered, my fingers curling into the fabric of his shirt.

"He didn't hurt you?"

"No. He just yelled at me."

Shame pulled me from the bathroom and down the hall to the living room. He sat me down on the couch and came back with the glass of wine I'd abandoned in the entrance-way. I took it and drank deeply. He sat down on the coffee table in front of me. I stopped drinking and glared at him.

"Get your ass off my coffee table. I just had it refinished."

"Shut up, Mercy, and finish your wine."

I finished the wine in one uncouth swallow and handed him the glass. "I don't need to be pampered. I'm fine."

"You beat a man with a bat in your bedroom, and you're fine?"

I shrugged. "I wish I hit him hard enough to break a few bones."

"Fuck, Mercy, you're killing me." He stood from the table and walked away. "It would be nice if you acted like a normal female for about twenty minutes. You know, cry and act scared so I can be the man."

I fell back against the couch. "You didn't get to act like a man when you *helped* Jeff into a cab?"

He looked at the floor and then shrugged. "That wasn't the same."

"Did you damage him permanently?"

Shame shrugged and looked back to me. "He may or may not be able to father children in the future."

I rubbed my face and shook my head. "Are all men like this?"

"The man violated you." His words came out through clenched teeth.

I flinched at his tone. "Yes, he did."

"And he did it again tonight." He looked around and sighed. "You've spent two years building a life where you felt safe, and then he showed up."

"And tore it to pieces," I admitted softly. "He doesn't matter, Shame. No matter how much he might have mattered in the past, he doesn't matter now. What he did to me was wrong, and the betrayal of it will linger in me all of my life, but it is in my past. It was wrong not to press charges against him when it happened; there is this place inside me where I'm full of guilt. I worry about the next woman he comes across that makes him feel inferior. I'd like to carve the word *rapist* into his forehead so that no woman will ever trust him again."

"You could still prosecute him for what he did."

"Yes."

"But you won't?"

"I won't."

"Why?" Shame asked so softly that I didn't realize for a minute that he'd spoken.

"Because it wouldn't give me justice. I can let myself wallow in what he did to me, or I can move on. It may sound cowardly. Hell, it may even be morally corrupt."

"What will give you justice, Mercy?"

"I don't know."

"Then why not report him to the police and take that step?"

"I left New York behind." I stood from the couch and walked to the other side of the room. "In labeling him a rapist, I would be telling the world that I was his victim."

"And you can't do that?"

"Not if my life depended on it."

The words fell hard between us. I met his gaze and saw the anger there. I knew he wasn't angry with me, but with a situation he'd never be able to control. I came with baggage that he hadn't expected.

"This is what I am, Shamus."

"I see that." He rubbed his head. "I knew you were a complicated piece of business before I ever took you to bed."

I laughed. "I don't think a man has ever called me a 'piece of business' before."

"Perhaps not to your face," he muttered.

I picked up my empty wineglass and walked toward the kitchen. "Would you like something to drink?"

"Hell, no."

I refilled my glass and turned to lean against the counter. I could see him from the kitchen; he paced back and forth a few times before he paused in the kitchen doorway. I waited.

"Come here, Mercy."

I placed the glass on the counter and walked to him. Taking the hand he offered, I shook a little as he pulled me close. Adrenaline, fear, and anger still simmered underneath my skin. I could feel the same restless energy in him. His hands moved down my back and slipped over my ass. My breath caught as he lifted me off the floor and coaxed my legs around his waist.

He placed me on the counter and touched my face carefully. "The first time I saw you, my insides tightened and pulled like I'd been struck. I didn't understand it, and I still don't. I want you, and if this is what you come with, I'm willing to work with it."

"Okay."

"I can't claim to be perfect." He brushed my hair back from my forehead and looked over my face. "I'll never look at you and see a victim. You survived a heinous act of violence. That's what you are, a survivor."

I sighed when he kissed my lips gently and then whispered my name as he moved his mouth along my jaw.

"I couldn't call for help," I said.

"Why not?"

Shaking, I pulled him close and buried my face in the side of his neck. "Because the one time I did, no one came."

Slipping out of my bed, I walked across the bedroom and into the bathroom. Grabbing my robe, I shrugged it on and tied the belt tight. The face staring back at me in the mirror didn't look scared. In fact, the woman in the mirror looked damn satisfied. I looked back to my bed and Shame, sprawled out across the mattress as if he owned it. He had come into my life so quickly, and I considered myself a very lucky woman.

I'd never known a man like him. I didn't know how to handle him. I picked up my brush and dragged it through my hair. Sleep and sex had made a mess of it. By the time I had all of the tangles out and had pulled it up in a clip, my bed was empty. I looked around the room and found Shame sitting in my bay window in a pair of boxers with Looney Toons characters all over them.

"Tell me the truth; you've got a relative with an obscure

sense of humor that sends you those things for Christmas, right?"

He laughed and shook his head. "I promise I buy them on my own. It's just one of those things you'll have to deal with."

As things went, it wasn't a bad one to deal with. I walked to him and sat down in the window beside him. "I know you're disappointed in my refusal to go back to New York and file charges against Jeff."

"Yes."

I was silent for a moment; I hadn't expected him to admit it. I sucked my bottom lip briefly but then released it. I found there was nothing else to say on that matter. Sighing, I stood and held out my hand. "Why don't you come back to bed and show me how much you like me?"

He stood and slipped his hand into mine. "Only if you promise not to make fun of my boxers."

I raised an eyebrow. "Darling, I wouldn't dream of it. In fact, I was thinking that perhaps I could buy you some, too. Do you have any boxers with The Little Mermaid on them?"

His fingers tightened in mine, and I found myself on my back in a few breathless seconds. Shame pressed me into the mattress and used his knee to spread my legs. "You'll be punished for that."

"What? You didn't like The Little Mermaid?" I asked softly.

I arched under him as he pressed his rapidly hardening cock against the silk of my robe. There was too much material between us. I spread my legs wider and strained against his hold. Trapped and fantastically aroused by his aggression, I waited for him to answer.

"What do you think?"

"Okay, how about his and hers boxers . . . you can be the Beast, and I can be Beauty." I bit down on my lip to keep from laughing.

"You think so?"

"Oh, yes," I nodded.

He pulled on the belt of the robe and pushed the material aside. With one hand he held both of my wrists above my head as his other hand slipped between my legs. My breath caught as Shame brushed his lips against mine before lowering his head to one breast. With his tongue, he flicked and teased the nipple until it was so painfully hard that each brush of his lips wrung a shuddering moan from my lips.

Everything about Shame was forcing me to alter my perceptions about myself and what I needed to survive. He released my hands as he lifted away from me, left the bed, and discarded his boxers. I watched him pull a condom out of the box he'd put on my nightstand with a grin and an anticipation that I didn't even try to hide. He came back to the bed, rolling the latex onto the thick length of his cock.

I rubbed my legs together as he put one knee on the bed and snagged one of my ankles. He pulled me gently across the bed to the edge of the mattress. Sitting up, I ran my hands over his thighs as I looked up and met his gaze. Intense need was a bare and honest reflection in his eyes.

Placing a small kiss on the flat plane of his stomach, I let my hands move to take both of his hands. Threading his fingers with mine, he pulled me to a standing position and took my place on the bed. Letting him guide me, I found myself sliding astride his thighs. He let my hands go and lifted me. I clasped his shoulders as he carefully lowered me onto his cock.

There it was, that hot bite of pleasure and pain that always came when I took him inside me. I let my head fall back as I sank onto him; the physical connection was deep and overwhelming. When I could, I lifted my head and met his eyes. The light from the bathroom gently revealed his face. He pulled me close as I started to gently rock on him.

I formed my hands into fists on his back to keep from digging into his skin with my nails. "I never understood."

"Understood what, baby?" His hands moved over my back then, gentle and thorough in their exploration.

"How something could be so good that it hurt."

He moved his hand between us, his thumb pressed against my clit, and every bit of control I thought I had fell away. The flush of orgasm was quick. Shaking, I barely recognized he'd stood from the bed until he laid me down on my back and started to push into me with deep, measured strokes.

CHAPTER 10

Simply put, I didn't have time for a disaster. But life has a habit of waiting until that moment when you can't take one more piece of straw and then it just jauntily tosses a two-hundred-pound bale your way. From the top of the stairs, I watched in wonder as Lisa Millhouse stood in front of James Brooks, repeatedly poking her finger against his chest. Language I normally reserved for being stuck in traffic poured out of her mouth, full of vehemence and conviction. If cursing someone out had been an Olympic event, I was sure Lisa could have medaled. Inclining my head, I looked to Jane. She was an avid audience member, and for once, I couldn't blame her. James and Lisa made an exciting and dynamic pair.

I repositioned my bag on my shoulder and strode forward with what I hoped was a tolerant smile on my face. "Good morning!"

Both of them turned on me, ready to bite, and then they both looked at the floor. Thankfully, reminded that they'd been giving fourteen people entirely too much entertainment, they were silent. I cleared my throat and motioned toward my office. "Why don't we continue this discussion in my office?"

Over my shoulder I shot Jane a look and gave her the universal *I need caffeine now* expression. She nodded and bolted away. I suppose she was relieved to be out of the line of fire.

I entered my office and shut the door. Lisa and James were both sitting in front of my desk, each on different ends of the three-chair arrangement. I took my time getting settled.

"Now." I leaned back in my chair and looked the two of them over. "Since I wasn't even aware the two of you knew each other, I can guarantee you that I have no clue what you could be arguing about. Without using the phrase 'he started it', Lisa, tell me what happened."

Lisa crossed her arms over her chest and glared at me for a long, silent moment. Then she sucked in a deep breath, bit down on her bottom lip, and burst out, "But he did start it!"

"The hell I did!"

"Mr. Brooks," I murmured. "It's not your turn to speak."

James slouched in his chair. "This isn't fair."

It was like talking to five-year-olds. "Is this conflict business, or is it personal?"

"Business," Lisa snapped.

"Personal," James corrected through clenched teeth.

Lisa blushed, and I started laughing. "I see, so the show you put on for the staff a few minutes ago was foreplay?"

Lisa stood. "You don't have to be insulting!"

"You're the one being insulting," James snapped in response.

"Oh, fuck you." Lisa stomped out of the office, slamming the door so hard the glass wall shook.

I looked at him. "Mr. Brooks, is it your intention to alienate all the artists who currently work with the gallery, or is it just Lisa you are out to vex?"

"This is none of your business, Mercy."

"Granted."

James rubbed his face and stood up. "The woman is an unreasonable wench. Most women don't mind being asked to dinner!"

I tapped one nail against the surface of my desk. "Did you

in any way imply that her status here at the gallery could be affected by having dinner with you?"

"Thanks," James muttered. "I had no idea you thought I was a sexist bastard."

"I didn't say that."

With exaggerated care, he took a deep breath and said, "No, Mercy, I didn't imply that her status at the gallery would be affected by going out with me." He glared at me as if he thought I didn't believe him. "Jane introduced us, and I told her that I liked the work I'd seen from her so far. She was here to discuss that high-school project with Jane. I horned in on their meeting because I was attracted to her. At the end of the meeting, Jane used her supersecret teleportation device to disappear." He shook his head and glanced at Jane, who had just returned with the coffee, which she put on my desk before retreating. "She has an amazing talent for that."

I laughed, understanding what he meant. "She's rather stealthy. So, what happened after Jane left the room?"

"I asked Lisa to have dinner with me, and I said I was interested in finding out more about the source of her inspiration. I've never seen a female sculptor with that kind of quiet passion and violence." He looked at me, and I knew that my thoughts were all over my face. "What?"

I sighed. "Lisa values her privacy."

"I can understand that."

"No." I shook my head. "Lisa is compulsive about her privacy. You'll have to mend this fence with her, and I honestly don't know how you can accomplish it." I looked out into the bull pen and sighed. "You might ask Shamus for some advice."

"I thought you and he were—"

"We are, but he's had a relationship with Lisa in the past. He knows her much better than either one of us." I watched James stand and shove his hands into his slacks. "And James,

I wouldn't suggest you call Lisa an unreasonable wench to her face. The woman does own a blowtorch."

James nodded and, with a small smile, left my office. I'll give Jane credit, she waited until he was down the stairs before she shot up out of her chair and hurried to the doorway of my office.

She shut the door, walked sedately to my desk, and then whispered in awe, "She called him everything but a cocksucker. She didn't even repeat herself."

Dropping my gaze to my desk, I tried to keep a straight face, but in the end, I lost the battle and laughed outright. Jane went and sat in the chair that James had abandoned. She waited until I was finished laughing before she continued.

She brushed her slacks as if she'd found lint on them and met my gaze. "They are so hot for each other."

I nodded and sighed. "Yeah, I noticed."

With his plans for hiring Jeff King thwarted, Milton had started in on the rest of the gallery. It took him about four hours to alienate nearly the entire administrative staff, and the whole day to get the best of the sales staff. Sales personnel are used to dealing with difficult people and have a high tolerance for bullshit. The women in the bull pen had taken to hiding in the bathroom in shifts of two or three. The two men who worked in the gallery hadn't been targeted by Milton, so they mostly ran interference for everyone else.

It was almost noon before Milton made his way to my office. He shut the door and tried to glare at me. He'd always struck me as an evil plus-sized leprechaun, though Lisa's garden-gnome idea had merit. Milton was a large man—it was his personality that made him seem so small and useless.

"What can I do for you, Milton?"

"Are you going to put Jane Tilwell in your place?"

"Yes."

"She isn't suited for the job."

"Ms. Tilwell holds degrees in both accounting and art history. She is perfect for this position."

"You'd be better off hiring Jeff King."

"No."

"I still have power around here."

"I don't consider the ability to bully and berate others power." I watched his face get red with anger, and I was surprised to see a tiny grimace of guilt. It rankled that he might be human after all.

He muttered something under his breath and left my office. I looked toward Jane's desk and found her on the phone. I sighed, and when she caught me looking, I motioned her to come in. I felt she had a right to be warned about Milton's irritation and his knowledge about her future at the gallery.

I'd forgotten about James Brooks until I got to Shame's gallery. Letting myself in with the key he'd slipped on my key ring, I hurried up the stairs and found James sitting in my red chair, a beer in one hand. He was waving his free hand around as he spoke. I frowned; I didn't like him sitting in my chair.

"The damn woman doesn't have a right to be so mean." His tone was petulant.

Shame laughed. "Women are possibly the cruelest creatures on earth. They all have too much attitude, but since they also have all the pussy, we just have to deal with it."

If I hadn't been carrying my big purse, I would have thrown it at him. "Mr. Montgomery."

He looked in my direction, pulled off his safety glasses, and shoved a tool in the pocket of his jeans. "Sweet Mercy, we were just talking about you."

I laughed and shook my head. "Why do I put up with you?"

"Ask me that again later. I'll be happy to remind you."

"I will." I raised an eyebrow and looked him over.

I started toward the second set of stairs, but stopped to pull off my shoes. "Are the two of you drinking your dinner?"

"He's drinking." Shame laughed and motioned to James, who was looking mournfully into an empty beer bottle. "I'm working. I ordered food. It should be here soon."

I nodded and paused at the feet of the stairs. "James."

He looked at me and offered me a smile. "Yes, Mercy?"

"You aren't going to find the answer to your question in the bottom of a bottle."

"I'm drowning my sorrows tonight. Tomorrow I'm going to practice groveling and begging. Then I'll go do it for real on Lisa's front porch."

I chuckled. "You might want to get some body armor."

"Excuse me?"

"At the very least, a cup would be a good investment."

As I started up the stairs, James asked Shame what I meant, and Shame laughed. "Lisa likes to shoot uninvited guests with a paint gun."

"Are you sure you want to go home?"

I laughed and let my fingers slip from Shame's as we came down the stairs into the gallery. Repositioning my purse, I nodded. "Yes. I have some things to take care of, and I have to prepare for a meeting with Samuel Castlemen. He'll be here in the morning."

Shame pulled me close and cupped my face with his hands. His mouth was soft and tender on mine. I could so easily blend into him, but after a moment I slipped away from him and out the door into the night. With one glance over my shoulder to give him a smile, I went to my car. He didn't shut the door until I was in my car with the doors locked.

The trip back to my apartment was spent mostly regretting

not getting laid before I left. At my apartment, I found a Post-it from the maintenance department in my building. They'd fixed the door and replaced my chain with a much stronger one. After entering my apartment and locking myself inside, I went to my answering machine out of habit and hit the button.

There was one message from my mother. Sighing, I listened to her talk about her recent shopping trip. She never stopped talking until my machine cut her off. "So, you just have to call me so I can come over and show you my new hat—it's a vibrant purple with a—"

The machine clicked, and I shook my head. I couldn't imagine what was on top of that hat, and a part of me really didn't want to find out. I pulled my hair down as the next message started. There was a loud sigh, and I looked at the machine and waited for Lisa to continue. She was the only one who sighed at my machine.

"Mercy, call me when you can. I've got the last piece ready for the gallery, and I'm digging a hole for a body. You just tell that asshole Brooks to stay in Boston, or he'll be in that hole."

I rubbed my face as I sat down, torn between laughing and crying. God, I hated the hostility she had for men. Hated it, understood it, and desperately wanted to help her heal it. Instinctually I understood that Lisa's past was horrifying, and I didn't want to know all the details. However, as her friend, I thought I had a responsibility to help her get on with her life.

The third message started. "Hey, Mercy. It's Jane. Look, when I came home this evening Jeff King was waiting on my doorstep. He's gone now."

I heard the machine click off as I hastily opened my front door and shoved my feet into a pair of shoes that I found by the entrance way. Once in my car, I forced myself to calm down and concentrate on driving. Jane only lived ten minutes from me by car, but it was the longest ten minutes of my life. I hated the thought of him being near her.

Her laughter and easygoing smile seemed so fragile then. I parked in front of her building and ran inside as if the devil were behind me.

Her apartment was on the first floor; I banged on her door and then tried the knob. "Jane?"

Locks clicked, and Jane opened the door. For a moment, I just stared at her. She was dressed in a nightshirt that read FUCK OFF, I DIDN'T ASK YOUR OPINION. She motioned me inside, her stuffed baby-seal-shaped house shoes flopping as she moved away from the door.

I said, "I haven't seen pink rollers like that since, well, in a long damn time."

She shot me dirty look and yawned. "What's up, Mercy?"

I swallowed hard and shook my head. "Jeff was here?"

"Yeah." She stretched and sat down on the couch. "I don't know what he wanted."

"How did you get him to leave?"

Jane snorted. "I pointed my 9mm at him."

Mouth hanging open, I sat down, and was pleased when my ass connected with a chair. "You have a gun?"

"Yes." She shrugged. "My brothers and my father are cops. In fact, I went through the academy and graduated myself."

"You could be a cop?"

"No, that's why I wear clothes that are too expensive and look at pretty things all day. I couldn't be a cop." She tipped over and lay across her couch. "Mercy, you woke me out of a dead sleep." Yawning again, she met my gaze across the room. "What's wrong?"

"Jeff came here."

Jane sat up abruptly. "You were worried about me."

I nodded and then shook my head. "Yes. I was worried. I

kept thinking that he had hurt you or that he would. It would have been my fault, Jane. If he'd hurt you . . ." I took a deep breath.

I stood and turned my back on her. A sigh turned into a sob. I didn't realize she'd left the couch until her arms came around me and she hugged me tightly. I accepted her embrace and then let her lead me back to the chair.

"All of this time, I considered what happened to me personal."

"It was personal."

"Yes." I nodded. "And it was something more. How could I think that his punishment was less important than my dignity?" My demand was met with silence. "I knew deep down that I had to make an effort to protect other women from him. At least if he were labeled as a sex offender, it would be something."

"Is it too late?"

I shook my head. "I don't think so." I glanced at her, saw the concern on her face. "I'm so sorry, Jane. Sorry that you were exposed to him, that he felt he could come here and threaten you because he couldn't get to me."

"He did get to you." Jane stood and walked away from me. "The moment I started leaving that message I realized that I had done exactly what he expected. He wasn't out to hurt me, Mercy; he was just using me and your affection for me as a weapon."

It had been effective. I looked at Jane then, saw her control and her ever-present I-can-do-anything attitude, and I knew that I no longer had the luxury of hiding behind my dignity. There was another woman out there somewhere; she would get in Jeff King's way, and he would hurt her if I didn't do something.

I stood. "I have to go."

"Mercy?"

I looked back to her. "I can't keep this inside any more."

She didn't follow immediately, so I waited outside her apartment door until I heard her turn the locks. Returning to my car, I dug through my purse for my wallet. There was a card in my wallet. I'd carried it since that first day in the hospital. I looked at it, tattered and worn just by being transferred from wallet to wallet as I changed purses.

For a moment, I just stared at the woman's name. Denise Moore. She'd been a detective when she'd attempted to interview me. I wondered what rank she held now, how far she had moved in her career. There were times when I lay in my bed thinking about her face as she'd turned to look at me in the doorway of the exam room. It looked as if she thought she could will me into telling her what she needed to know.

I picked up my cell phone and dialed the number she'd scrawled on the back before I could change my mind. It rang several times, and then a groggy female voice answered. I swallowed hard and lowered my head as she said hello for the fourth time.

"My name is Mercy Rothell."

There was a long moment of silence, and then she cleared her throat. I could hear her moving around as if she were leaving her bed. "What can I do to help you, Mercy?"

"You can tell me it's not too late to make the man who raped me pay for it."

"How long ago was it?"

"Roughly two years."

"Did you file a report at the time?"

"Yes, I made a statement and submitted to a rape exam, but in the end I didn't press charges." I closed my eyes and lowered my head until it rested against the wheel. "I thought that if I tried to forget about it, that it would go away. I thought he wouldn't matter."

"I understand."

"Will filing charges change anything?"

"It's a step toward justice, Mercy. Once you take that step, you'll begin to heal again. I know you've spent a lot of time rebuilding what you lost." She sighed. "What helped you make this decision?"

"He's invading my life. He broke into my apartment, and this evening he visited a close friend."

"Where are you?"

"At the moment or geographically?"

She laughed; it was a soft, pretty sound that I enjoyed. I felt my body relax, and my stomach slowly start to let go of the knots that had been there for more than hour. "I'm in Boston. I'm currently in my car on my cell phone."

"Go home."

"I don't feel safe there."

"Is there a place where you feel safe?"

"Yes."

"Go there, Mercy. Seek sanctuary from this, and in the morning, I want you to come to New York. We'll start the paperwork, and we'll make this happen for you. Fortunately for you, I am someone who never gives up. Every rape I've ever been assigned has a file with all the evidence I could gather, even the ones who later chose not to file a complaint."

"How do you do what you do?"

"I remember that what I do might keep one victim out of harm's way."

"I'll book a flight to New York and call you back as soon as I know when I can be there."

When I got out of my car, the gallery door was opening. I paused and watched Shame as he looked around and spotted me. He shoved his keys into his pocket and walked toward me. I no longer wondered why going to him when I was upset seemed like the right thing to do, it just was.

"Where have you been?"

I motioned to my car. "Sitting in my car."

He offered me his hand and smiled when I took it. "Jane called me more than an hour ago. Why didn't you pick up your cell?"

"The last call I made killed the battery."

He said nothing as he pulled me along behind him. In the gallery, he locked the door and turned to me. Shaking, I let him draw me close, his mouth grazing my jaw before slipping down my neck to my shoulder. I dug my fingers into his arms as I pulled him closer. Desperate need seemed to bleed out between us. Sinking my teeth into the flesh of his neck, my hands dropped to his waist, and I tugged at the jeans he hadn't bothered to belt. He pulled at my blouse, revealing the skin of my shoulder. I felt his teeth graze the flesh, and I curled my fingers against him. Hot, desperate lust pushed at my will.

The button and zipper of his jeans gave way, and I slipped my hand inside. His cock stirred against my hand, warm and rapidly hardening. I let him go reluctantly when he pulled my shirt out of the waistband of my slacks. Shoving my shoes off, I pulled the shirt over my head, dropped it on the floor, and watched him with half-closed eyes as he followed my example.

With careful hands, he pulled me to him and maneuvered us toward the stairs. I knew we weren't going to make it up to the top of them. Sucking in a breath of approval, I nodded as he sat down and pulled me into his lap. I pressed my breasts against his chest and took his mouth in the kind of kiss that demanded about a thousand things. I knew he'd give me everything I needed, and exactly what I wanted.

I stroked his cock and pressed it against my belly as his hands moved down my back to my ass. Fleetingly I thought about a condom, but knew we were beyond searching one out. He lifted me, and I arched in his arms as I slid down onto his cock. Hot and full, the sting of taking him inside was the most pleasure I'd ever known. As always, the pressure of his cock inside me reminded me of how empty I was without him. Wrapping my arms around his neck, I rocked on him.

"Easy," he whispered against my throat. "Just relax, Mercy."

I started to shake against him and buried my face in the side of his neck. "I can't."

He laughed softly, dragging his hands down my back in a way that should have been soothing, but wasn't. His hands felt rough and inexperienced, I understood what he meant then. I'd finally managed to reduce him to the same state he so often left me in. Gripping his shoulders, I met his gaze and saw the raw state of his arousal. The near violence of our need was pushing past any civilized veil we had in place.

He stood, gripping me tightly. I clung and gasped when he lowered me to the glossy wood floor of his gallery. The wood was unyielding and hard beneath me, and he was just as relentless on top of me. With his hands planted on either side of my head, the rest of his body pushed heavy and demanding against me.

"Shame."

"Hold on, Mercy."

It was all I could do. I held on to to him and let go of everything else. The ache built inside me, each thrust of his cock a heady reminder of the union I had craved. The light from the stairs fell across us, highlighting the paleness of my skin against the darkness of his. I loved the feel of him and the look of him. He was so beautiful, and in that hot, unspeakable instant, I understood that I truly had been waiting for him.

An orgasm rushed against my clit, and I arched hard, deep from the floor. My nails dug into his back, and tears streamed down my face, his name a litany pouring from my mouth. Slick with sweat, our bodies continued to glide against each other. I felt the fleeting heat of his seed and closed my eyes at the primal sensation it woke in me.

EPILOGUE

Two Months Later

"What's happening in New York?" Lesley asked.

"Jeff has an attorney, and he's claiming our encounter was consensual. The DA took one look at the pictures of me and filed charges." I grimaced. "I hadn't seen the pictures until then. I don't remember being so bruised. The indictment is pending, but they seem confident that it will go to trial."

Pulling my legs up in the recliner, I shrugged. "I want to feel good about what I'm doing. For a while there I felt guilty for it, and I know that sounds crazy. He's threatened to file a civil suit against me for defamation of character."

"He lost his job, right?"

Sighing, I nodded. "He was suspended from the museum pending the outcome of the case. Edward's official statement indicated that he would not place the female personnel of the museum knowingly at risk."

"Why the guilt?"

"I'm ruining his life." The admission wasn't something that made me feel guilty, at least not any more. "I want to believe that he made a mistake, that it isn't something he'd ever do again. But I don't."

"How are things at the gallery?"

Grimacing, I shook my head. "Once the staff got wind of what happened to me in New York, they started to treat me like I was breakable." Sighing, I tried to think about how I felt in the gallery. "I resented their pity, but then I realized that they really didn't pity me. They were just afraid. Most of the gallery employees are female. Every time they see me, they're reminded that rape isn't a distant crime that won't ever touch them." I hated being a statistic, but I was. *Every two minutes a woman is raped in America.* The DA in New York had told me that. I could still hear the words coming out of his mouth, anger and conviction bleeding into his voice. "I'm not a number."

"No."

"Now that I'm Director, I have a lot more on my plate. Every time I turn around I have a new artist wanting to be seen, or an agent trying to talk me into a show. It's a different world."

And it was. Jane was blossoming in her role as Assistant Director and had taken on the high-school project. It was going beautifully. All of the young energy in the gallery was amazing and refreshing.

I walked around the alabaster and pulled the sheet free. Startled, I could only stare. He was done. The statue already gleamed with polish. I touched the smooth surface of my face and then walked around to view the back. As most women would do, I checked out what was visible of my ass on the statue and felt relieved that it didn't look too big.

"What do you think?"

"I never knew I could be this naked," I responded honestly, walking back around to view my face. "Is this really what you see when look at me?"

"Yes, I see a powerful and amazing woman." He came to me and pulled me into his arms. "I learned something about you, Mercy."

"What is that?"

"Undressing you had nothing to do with getting you out of your clothes." He kissed my forehead and sighed. "However, the bronze will be the twenty-third piece for the Holman show. No one gets to see you this naked but me."

I laughed and looked to the woman in the gleaming alabaster. "It's the most naked I've ever been."

He pulled me closer and wrapped him arms around me. "How'd things go with Lesley?"

"Good." My therapy sessions weren't something I discussed a great deal, and Shame accepted that private part of me with grace. The lack of pressure and his complete acceptance of me were always sources of wonder.

Looking back at the statue, I was floored by the honesty of it. Every emotion I had was there, every victory and every tragedy bared before the world. I didn't feel invaded, though I supposed that some people would have. I felt liberated by it, set free from all of the things I'd held close for longer than I cared to think about. However, more than my past was there; my future was there too. My hope and the love I'd never expressed for him showed in my face.

"It's true," I said finally.

"I know."

Anyone else would have said the words, I didn't. He'd seen it in me before I'd even let myself acknowledge it. He saw hope in me before I even tried to have it. I would keep my words, at least for a little while. His hands brushed over my back and tugged at my shirt.

"What are doing?"

"I would think that would be obvious." He carefully pulled my shirt completely free from my slacks. "Don't ruin my fantasy. If you can't contribute to it, just be quiet."

I laughed. Having my words thrown back in my face normally pissed me off. I curled my fingers into the front of his jeans and pulled at him. "I can make contributions the likes of which have never been seen by a mere man."

"Such contributions would be aptly rewarded," he promised as he gently but firmly guided me toward his favorite chair.

God, I love that red chair.

The moon is out! The beast is on the prowl!
Turn the page for a peek at SEXY BEAST!

Available now . . .

1

One moment, she was a tall, elegantly dressed African American woman with long, darkly waving hair and eyes of brilliant amber. In less than a heartbeat, her dress lay on the redwood deck in a tumbled shimmer of blue satin. The woman had become the wolf, amber eyes glinting angrily in the last dying rays of the sun, canines glimmering like ivory blades. With a single low growl and a flick of her tail, she leapt over the deck railing and raced through the damp meadow.

Anton Cheval threw back his head and laughed. Keisha hated to lose an argument, any argument.

"You gonna let her get away with this?"

Anton turned to the couple sitting behind him, snuggled close together on the big porch swing.

Grinning broadly, Stefan Aragat lifted his wine glass. "She *is* your mate. You better chase her down. We'd help, but Xandi and I plan to enjoy the sunset before we run."

Anton glared at Stefan for a brief moment, then shook his head in resignation. Stefan was right. If he didn't chase after Keisha and work this out now, he'd never hear the end of it.

Anton's abrupt shift from human to wolf left his clothing in a messy pile on the deck. So unlike him, he thought, not to remember to undress first and fold everything neatly. He glanced once more at the dark pants and black cashmere sweater lying in an untidy heap, then cleared the deck railing and the garden beyond in a single bound.

Maybe laughter hadn't been his best response.

Only Keisha could leave him so flustered.

Or so turned on.

Anton's powerful forelegs stretched out and he gathered speed with each thrust of his haunches, but his mind was not entirely the wolf. No, he was reacting like a very protective male, no matter the species, and he knew it irritated the hell out of his alpha mate.

It didn't matter. He was not, under any circumstances, going to allow her to return to San Francisco by herself. It went against all he stood for, all that the Chanku were. Their strength lay in the pack, not in the individual.

The memorial garden Keisha had designed for Golden Gate Park was moving forward according to schedule. She'd made enough trips, accompanied by either Anton or Stefan, to ensure everything would be perfect for the dedication. There was no reason she needed to go back early.

Not with that damned tabloid reporter, Carl Burns, once more on her trail.

Anton snarled and almost missed the leap across a small, partially frozen stream. The mere thought of the persistent reporter raised his hackles, made his heart race faster, his blood run hotter.

Burns was the one man who could expose them, the one person who not only suspected the existence of Chanku, but had actually witnessed Keisha's shift from woman to wolf.

Anton knew his ability to mesmerize was extraordinary, but even he had his limits. He'd hoped the mind-job he'd done on the tabloid reporter would erase the smut-peddler's memories of Keisha for a longer time than they had, but the bastard had suddenly reappeared in their lives on Keisha's last trip to the city.

Why hadn't Keisha let Anton file harassment charges? Carl Burns was a menace, a threat not only to Anton's mate but to the pack as a whole.

No matter. Anton's meetings in Boston would be over in less than a week and they could make the trip west together. He had a lot of money riding on this latest investment. Stefan was learning the business, but he wasn't up to handling an entire board of directors for a multi-national company all by himself.

Following the frosty trail with his wolven mind, working through the problems concerning Keisha with his human side, Anton loped across the familiar ground. He still wasn't certain what he could say to make her wait, but somehow he would convince her of the danger.

He had to.

Danger!

Keisha's warning hit him like a solid object. Another scent assaulted his sensitive nostrils. Anton ducked low, twisted and slipped off the trail.

Male. Not Chanku. Human male. More than one, very close. Anton raised his nose and sniffed the air. He scented excitement, fear and the sour sweat of unwashed human.

Keisha's scent was strongest, to the right.

Pain. Anger. Fear.

Her emotions washed over him, impossible to understand, beyond speech, beyond coherent thought. Anton veered off the main trail and, keeping his body low to the ground, raced down a narrow, bramble-filled ditch. Tufts of dark hair clung to some of the thorns. He scented blood and his hackles rose. Either she was so pissed she was ignoring the thorns, or something—someone—had hurt her.

All thoughts of meetings, investments, humanity, evaporated. Pure wolven rage filled Anton's heart, seared his thoughts. His lips curled back in a dark snarl, exposing sharp canines.

Anton!

Keisha's mental cry, clear now, ringing true as a bell in his mind, sent ice running through his veins.

Anton! Take care! Poachers. Armed with crossbows.

He skidded to a halt, one foot raised, his sensitive nose finding Keisha's scent, smelling blood along with her unique, feminine fragrance, pinpointing her location. At the same time, he reached out with his thoughts to touch Stefan and Xandi.

The connection was instantaneous, their response immediate. Satisfied, Anton raced toward his mate. *I'm coming. Are you hurt?*

Just grazed. Stay low. Can you reach Stefan? I can't find him.

I've already contacted him. He's on his way. He'll bring the four-wheeler and he's armed. Xandi's called the sheriff. Where are the poachers?

Near the pond. They've built a blind at the far end, above the beaver dam.

Anton passed the information on to Stefan. Scanned the thick underbrush along the near edge of the pond. Keisha's scent and the odor of fresh blood were strong, her fear and anger a palpable thing. *Where are you?*

Near the birch stand. Low, in the bramble patch.

He found her there, curled into a tight ball, her blood dripping steadily into the remnants of one last patch of crusty snow. She'd packed the shallow wound in her shoulder with ice, at least as well as she could in wolven form. Tiny crystals tinged with blood clung to the stiff whiskers along her muzzle.

Anton inspected the wound, licked the matted fur around it, grabbed a mouthful of ice and pushed it tightly against the seeping gash. Thank goodness, it didn't appear life threatening.

He licked Keisha's muzzle, wiping away the bloody snow with a careful swipe of his tongue. *I should kill them. They need to die.* Anton's thought ended on a snarl of pure rage.

No, you should have them arrested. They're idiots. Let the law deal with them.

Keisha's calm statement helped slow his racing heart. Still, he growled, unwilling to concede too easily. *I will, but I don't have to like it. I'd rather kill them.*

Keisha raised her head and glowered at him through eyes shimmering with pain. Sighing, Anton nuzzled her once more and waited impatiently for Stefan to arrive with clothing for both of them . . . hopefully before Xandi brought the sheriff.

This made the third set of poachers on their land this season—all of them hunting wolves.

Naked, Keisha sat on the toilet seat lid, hunched over in pain and seething with anger while Anton cleaned the shallow gash across her left shoulder. Her body trembled, a delayed reaction to the shooting.

Stefan and Xandi would be back later. They'd followed the sheriff into town to give more of a statement after one of his deputies had taken Keisha and Anton's. Now, alone here with Anton, Keisha felt the full impact of the night's attack.

"Are you sure you don't want to see the doctor?" Anton's fingers caught her gently under the chin and lifted, forced her to face him. "It's not all that deep, but it could leave a scar."

"Then it leaves a scar. I'll be fine. Damn them. I hope they rot in jail." Her voice shook, but it was rage, not pain that had her hanging on the edge of tears. "Somebody put them up to this. They were too stupid to come here on their own. I just know it."

Anton placed a gentle kiss on her lips. "I agree. I just wish we knew who it was. I doubt those men know enough to shed any light on the situation. Unfortunately, I imagine an attorney will have them out of jail in a few hours."

"Well, I'll be long gone. I'm planning to leave for San Francisco the day after tomorrow. I've already got my flight arranged." Keisha tilted her head, daring him, waiting for his argument. Anton's eyes narrowed but he kept his mouth shut. Instead, he carefully bandaged Keisha's wound and drew her slowly into his arms.

She went willingly, inhaling the musky scent that was all Anton's, reveling in the strength of his embrace, the deep sense of love and safety that surrounded him. It would be so easy to lose herself in Anton's arms, to forget the memorial, the dedication, the fact that someone hunted her as if she were nothing more than a wild beast.

So easy to forget the danger when Anton held her tight.

"I was terrified when I heard your warning of danger, when I sensed your fear." Anton's voice cracked on the words and a deep shudder passed through his body. Keisha clung to him, suddenly awash with guilt. She'd been thinking only of herself, of her desire to see the job through. What if it had been Anton wounded today? What if she'd followed his blood on the trail? Found him curled up in a ball of pain, hurting and frightened?

Could she have controlled her rage as well as Anton did? Would she have even tried? It hit her like an epiphany, the explosive awareness of how wild her nature had become since embracing her Chanku heritage. Keisha accepted a new reality—if Anton had been the one injured, the two shooters wouldn't have survived long enough to go to jail. She'd killed men before. As much as she abhorred violence, she could do it again if her mate were threatened.

It took her a moment to tamp down the rush of bloodlust that almost swamped her. Finally, she swallowed back a growl and nuzzled close to Anton's chest. "I wasn't afraid, not once

I knew you were close." She wrapped her arms around his neck and rose up on her toes to kiss him. "I'm never afraid when you're with me."

Anton groaned, the sound a sensual rumble against her breasts. Keisha whimpered, a tiny, needy sound deep in her throat. She inhaled his scent, drawing strength from his warmth and innate power. She rocked her hips close to his, rubbed her mons over the smooth fabric of his pants.

Anton groaned, then kissed her hard, his tongue plundering, his teeth scraping her lips, along her jaw, nipping at her with a wild frenzy. His lips demanded. His hands raced across her back, over her breasts, swept down to her buttocks where he grabbed her with bruising strength and pressed her body closer to his.

Caught in his feverish desire, Keisha cried out against his mouth. She felt the heat of his erection through his black chinos, the hard edge of his belt buckle abrading her belly. The flap of fabric over his bulging zipper pressed against her swollen clit. His tongue found its way once more between her lips and he caught her up in a swift and carnal rhythm, plunging into her mouth, lifting her body hard against his.

She wrapped her legs around his waist and pressed her pussy close against his straining cock, but it wasn't enough, not nearly enough to soothe the fire raging hot and wild inside.

Keisha writhed in Anton's powerful grasp, all the anger and pain, the fear and frustration of the past few hours coalescing into heat and passion, need of an almost feral intensity, driving her heart, inflating her lungs, making her gasp as if she'd run miles. Keisha lowered her legs, planted her feet firmly on the tile floor and let go of Anton's neck, then grabbed at the hem of his sweater. She raked her fingernails over his ribs as she tugged the garment past his head.

The moment he shed the sweater, Anton dragged her

against him for a deep, tongue-twisting, mind-searing kiss. Gasping for air, he backed away and stared deeply into her eyes, his nostrils flaring, his dark pupils narrow slits, dark shards of obsidian surrounded in amber.

Keisha reached for his thoughts and found them blocked, surrounded by something dark and impenetrable. Whatever he felt for her, whatever he thought of her, remained hidden behind those watchful eyes.

Fingers trembling, Keisha raised her right hand and touched Anton's cheek. He turned and kissed her palm, groaning once again. She felt the press of his lips all the way to her womb. The tight clenching of her vaginal walls, the rush of welcoming fluids, the ache deep within her gut wrung a cry from her lips and she thrust her breasts against his bare chest, rubbing her sensitive nipples in the thick mat of his dark hair.

Anton nipped her palm, took a deep breath, then grabbed Keisha by the hips and spun her around, pressing her belly against the cool tile surrounding the bathroom sink. Shoving the First Aid kit aside, she spread her palms wide and braced herself on the counter. With his left hand in the small of her back holding her down, Anton found her wet and waiting pussy with the fingers of his right.

He thrust two fingers, then three inside, slipping easily into her drenched pussy, stroking her inner walls, trailing his thumb lightly across her anus, then pressing harder, finding entrance there as well.

She felt the tight muscle relax, then close once more around the base of his thumb as he once again found a seductive rhythm. In, out, penetrating both passages, slow and deep, his thumb pressing against his fingers through the thin wall of sensitive flesh inside her body.

Gasping for air, Keisha spread her legs even wider, flattening her belly hard against the tile. Once more she tried to reach Anton's thoughts.

Still she found them closed to her.

Her climax was rushing forward, but she heard the sound of his zipper, the rustle of cloth and Anton's body was there, the broad head of his cock pressing hard against her wet and waiting pussy, her swollen and sensitive lips parting, giving Anton passage.

His body, but not his thoughts. His skill as a lover, but not his love. Suddenly Keisha understood as awareness flooded her mind, left her soul wanting, her heart hurting.

This was not an act of love at all, at least not love as Keisha expected it. No. This was something darker, something ancient and ritualistic.

This was something she must fight or accept, the way of Chanku.

The way of the alpha male subduing his bitch.

Pressing Keisha flush against the smooth tile until her breasts were flattened and her cheek rested on the hard surface, Anton thrust hard and fast, establishing his dominance, his power and physical strength over his mate.

Keisha thought to struggle, then accepted. He might be physically stronger, yet she was the winner, the one who cried out in mindless pleasure when Anton pumped his seed into her, the one who begged for more, then milked him with powerful muscles until his legs quivered and he leaned across her back to keep from falling to the floor.

The one who opened her mind at the point of climax and found his waiting—conscience-stricken, apologetic and remorseful beyond description.

Each harsh breath forced his chest against her back and her tight vaginal muscles continued their steady contraction and release around his shrinking cock.

Anton sensed no anger from her, no fear, no emotion beyond love and her underlying compassion.

He couldn't believe what he'd just done! This was no better than rape, this harsh and forced lovemaking . . . no, he couldn't begin to call it lovemaking. Keisha would never forgive him.

She shouldn't forgive him.

How would he go on living if she didn't?

He raised his head, spread his palms out on the cool tile to separate himself from Keisha's warm body.

"No. Please. Not yet." She turned and smiled at him. "Damn. You feel too good inside me. Don't go yet."

"But . . . ?" Anton frowned. "You're not . . . ?"

"Not what? Pissed?" She grinned, a lopsided smile that tore at his heart. "A little. On the other hand, if I'd wanted to stop you, all I needed to do was tell you to stop, right?"

He thought about that a minute. He would have quit in a heartbeat, no matter how angry, if he'd thought she wanted him to. "Okay, that's true, but . . ."

Keisha reached up and brushed her knuckles across his chin. "I didn't ask you to stop, Anton. I love you. We were both a bit overdosed on adrenaline. Do you love me?"

You know I do. I love you more than life itself.

Then why did you block your thoughts?

Anton sighed, then slowly withdrew from her body. He grabbed a yellow washcloth, held it under running water a moment, then wrung it out and handed it to Keisha. She turned around, leaned against the counter where they'd just had the most amazing sexual encounter, and unselfconsciously began to clean the semen and fluids from between her legs.

Anton watched her for a moment, mesmerized by the sweep of the damp yellow cloth against her dark skin and realized he wanted her again. He would always want her. He sighed, took the washcloth after she rinsed it in the sink and held it. "I didn't want you to see an anger I couldn't fully comprehend, didn't want you to think less of me, to realize I can't always control the beast inside."

Keisha grinned, grabbed the washcloth hanging limply in his hand and began to wash his no longer limp cock. "You control the beast admirably, my love. Just don't try to control me."

She raised her head and gazed at him for a long moment. Anton watched her perfect breasts rise and fall with each breath she took, then looked up, into her eyes. "If you do," she said, and her voice was tight with emotion, "you'll lose me forever."

Turn the page for a sneak peek at AFTER HOURS, coming in April 2006 from Aphrodisia!

1

There was something to be said about the way a woman danced. Between her body-hugging, short red dress and the arousing way she twisted her sleek curves, the woman who currently held Brendan Jordan's attention seemed to be saying "do me" loud enough to be heard halfway across the hotel reception hall.

He glanced over at Mike Donovan, his one-time college roommate and the newest victim of matrimony, then nodded toward the blonde.

From his seat next to Brendan at the head table, Mike followed Brendan's gaze. His grin turned from one of newly married idiocy to that of male understanding. "Pretty incredible, isn't she?" he asked loudly, to be heard over the blaring music.

Drool-worthy was a more suitable way to describe her. Only, Brendan didn't drool over women. If anything, the situation was reversed. They gave him the hot, hungry, fuck-me looks that made it clear what they wanted even before they approached. And, if they were lucky, he gave it to them.

The blonde wasn't drooling over him. Judging by the dreamy expression that tugged her slightly too wide mouth into one of the sexier smiles he'd seen, she wasn't even aware there were other people in the room.

Brendan was aware, however. Aware of how damned long he'd been sitting there ogling her. Looking away, he took a long pull from his beer. He set the bottle back on the table before nonchalantly asking, "So, who is she?"

Mike's eyebrows rose. "You haven't met Jilly?"

"That's her name?" Brendan gave the woman an assessing look. Jilly didn't sound right. With breasts plump enough to fill his hands and a curvy ass that had the bulk of his blood firing straight to his dick, she deserved a far more sensual name.

"I'd just assumed with your new jo—"

Brendan glanced back at Mike. "My what?"

Mike's gaze clouded over. After a few seconds, his grin returned—a little too deviously, in Brendan's mind. Mike used to grin like that back in college, just before he pulled the kind of shit that ended up getting both of them in trouble.

"Never mind what I was about to say." Mike pushed his chair back from the table. "Let me do the honors of introducing you."

Brendan pushed back his own chair and stood. The blonde might not be eyeing him over the way he felt various other women doing, but that didn't mean he needed Mike's help in getting her to talk to him. There was a reason he'd earned the title of "The Midwest's Most Eligible Bachelor" from *People* magazine. That reason wasn't due to shyness around women, knockouts or otherwise. It was because of his money and heritage and, more than that, his business savvy. He'd opted to take a break from the financial aspects of business and try his hand at the advertising end of things less than two years ago. Already he was rising up the corporate ladder with relative ease.

"Thanks for the offer," he said to Mike, "but I can handle things from here."

"Sure thing. Just let me know when you need help."

Brendan laughed at the absurdity of the statement. They might share a passion, and even wisdom, for success, but they sure as hell didn't for females. Mike's knowledge of women could fit into a thimble. If it hadn't been for Brendan literally pushing him in his new wife's direction, the man would still be single.

Single, free and happy.

Guilt edged through Brendan, quickly fading when he noted the nauseatingly doting smile Mike shot his bride's way. Nothing to feel guilty about there, just as there was nothing to be learned. "The day I need help with women from you, Donovan, is the day I'll have truly sunk to an all-new low."

Mike glanced back at him, humor lighting his eyes. "Hey, whatever you say, man. Just remember you said that come Monday."

What was Monday? The day he started in on his latest career venture with the high-power, Atlanta-based advertising firm Neilson & Sons, but what did that have to do with the she-devil working her magic on the dance floor?

Whatever it was, it wasn't important enough to stay in his mind and, therefore, not important enough to worry over.

With a last look at Mike, whose attention was again on his wife, Brendan started across the room. He stopped on the edge of the light-brightened dance floor where a mass of females and a handful of males worked their bodies in a number of interesting moves. None quite so interesting as Jilly's, however.

Her profile was to Brendan, but he could still make out far more than he'd been able to back at the table. Honey-blond hair framed an expressive face and hung midway down her back in loose waves. Full breasts pressed against the snug bodice of her short, sequined dress as her nicely rounded ass swayed seductively in time with the music. Black high-heels streamlined long, slender legs encased in sheer stockings. While her eyes were closed, the sultry look on her face said plenty.

So did the arousal in his tuxedo pants that turned his cock from slightly hard with simple interest to rock-solid and throbbing.

There was something about her. Something he needed to

discover before this night was over, or, at the very least, some-thing he needed to uncover by way of removing the layers of silk, sequins and nylon that hid the lush body beneath.

Not about to stand by and wait for her to open her eyes, Brendan moved onto the dance floor and through a sea of thriving bodies to the one he ached to touch.

Jillian Lowery's pulse went from a happily fast beat to all-out chaos in two seconds flat. A hand settled over her belly—a hand that she didn't need to look down at to know was large and masculine. If the sudden throbbing between her thighs that came with the hot breath caressing her neck and the languorous movements against her backside were any sign, the owner of that hand knew exactly what he was doing.

She should stop his highly suggestive and far too intimate moves, whoever he was. Any other day she would. Today wasn't a normal day. Today was the first time in a very long while that she wasn't surrounded by colleagues and clients alike who'd come to respect her cool, professional demeanor. Today the subdued wilder side of Jillian had a chance to come out and play. After today, that Jillian would have to go back into hiding until some unknown time in the future.

She should stop him, but she wasn't going to. Not yet any-way.

Summoning nerves she'd forgotten she possessed, Jillian covered the stranger's hand with her own and ground her bot-tom against her dance partner's groin. The hand tightened at her waist and a low growl drifted to her ears. The animalistic sound would have been enough to bring too-long-denied hunger swelling to life. The length of an erection pressed against her buttocks was more than enough. Wetness gathered in her panties and her pulse threatened to beat out of control.

The hand beneath hers slid lower, down the sequined silk of her dress, and his palm turned and molded itself to the slight curve of her mound. The breath snagged in her throat. Perspiration gathered on her flushed skin. Her hips reacted out of instinct, grinding against that hot, weighty touch.

Restlessness screamed through Jillian, further moistening her panties with the juices of arousal, making her want in a way she hadn't experienced in years. Maybe ever.

Need egged her on, shut out all thoughts of their surroundings, of the flashing lights and thundering music. Jillian tightened her hold on his hand, urging it to press harder, silently begging him to go farther. To push her dress aside and sink his fingers deep into her aching pussy, thrusting them in and out until she cruised past the limits of ecstasy and there could be no stopping her mindless screams of release.

He pressed the slightest bit harder. Her clit throbbed. She mewled deep in her throat. "Oh, yes. God, please . . ."

She wanted so badly.

Wanted to forget about being the consummate business-woman. Wanted to let go and be the fun-loving, carefree woman she'd left behind four years ago. Wanted to experience satisfaction once this decade that didn't have anything to do with landing another prestigious client en route to obtaining her dream job.

"I'd love to please you, Jilly, but we're on a dance floor, sweetheart. As crowded as it is, the song's going to end soon and everyone's going to see where my hand's at."

The thickly spoken words drifted to her ears, reflecting appetite as well as humor. Jillian heard both, but it was the truth that pulled her from the sensual haze, the truth of how much she'd allowed herself to forget the mistakes of the past and let herself go. Panic assailed her, tightening her limbs and tamping back the raw desire coiled to life in her belly and burning like a wildfire of need deep in her core. Her grinding moves came to an abrupt halt as judgment returned to taunt her.

Oh, God, what the hell had she been thinking?

She had to stop this. Had to explain that she'd allowed the music to carry her away and act completely shameless with a man she had yet to set eyes on.

But how?

And did she honestly want to?

Anxiety ate at her, but so did the scintillating thrill of doing the kind of daring thing she hadn't done in years. The kind of thing she would never do with or around those who knew her as Jillian the Professional.

The magical hand that had spun warmth and wetness in her with barely more than a touch lifted away. The discontented whimper that broke from her lips answered her earlier question. She didn't want to end this. Only, judging by the fact that her dance partner had let her go, he did.

Dejection filled her for one gloomy second, and then he caught her hand in his and twirled her. She landed awkwardly against a wide, hard chest and swallowed back a breath of mixed shock and elation. He wasn't dismissing her, just changing course as the music dictated.

The flashing overhead lights gave way to the soft glow of candles arranged throughout the reception hall. A slow melody drifted from the front of the room, a mesmerizing song that had nothing on the gripping heat in the stranger's eyes.

They were dark—maybe brown or deep blue; Jillian couldn't tell in the dim lighting. She could tell other things, like his build. He had a good six inches on her five-foot-seven frame, and, if the feel of his body against hers was any sign, he was both muscular and lean. Thick, dark hair framed an angular face that sported a touch of five-o'clock shadow. Full lips hovered over hers as if they might advance at any moment.

Her mind cleared with that last thought and a fresh dose of heat coursed through her. He was yummy, but he was also vaguely familiar. From the wedding party, yes, but for some other reason. Some reason she prayed had nothing to do with business.

"You're a friend of Mike's?" she asked.

He twined her arms around his neck, then placed his own at her waist as they fell into a slow dance. A lazy smile tugged at his lips. "From college, yes."

He was educated, whoever he was. Not that education mattered for what she wanted to do with him, but . . . What she wanted to do with him? What did she want to do? Okay, have a night of wild and kinky sex—that much was a given, from the shockingly hard points of her nipples to the cream that seeped between her thighs—but did she dare? Not without a little more information.

Jillian didn't want to know him well, just as she didn't want him to know her well. Too much information could lead to potential future problems. A few details were important, though. For starters, if he was married.

But, no, he wasn't married. Mike might only know Jillian through his new wife, Molly, but he still wouldn't allow a married man to come on to her. "What would Mike say if I asked about you?"

The stranger's smile kicked higher. His fingers began a rhythm at her waist that was both featherlight and amazingly distracting. "That I love a good challenge and know how to leave a woman with a smile."

The cockiness of the answer probably should have made her have second thoughts. Instead, she laughed and smiled back. God, how she missed bantering for the hell of it. "So, you're a womanizer?"

"Is that what it sounded like?"

"Is that how it is?"

Seconds ticked by, and Jillion anxiously waited for his response. It came in actions instead of words. His fingers moved higher, along her thinly clothed sides, to graze the outer swell of her breasts. He applied the slightest bit of pressure and her nipples pulsed for his touch.

That dangerously sexy mouth of his curved once more.

His eyes showed amusement that ensured he knew the effect he was having on her. It was tempting to turn away and reject him and the arrogance he gave off as far as his sexual appeal was concerned. She might have, too, if at that moment his thumb didn't reach out to stroke the underside of her breast, the pad moving in a leisurely circle that had every one of her nerves at attention.

She bit back a sigh that he would move inward, closer to her straining nipple. There was no need to sigh, no need to beg. She could feel his swollen cock cradled against her belly. He wanted her. All she had to do was say she wanted him, too, and they would be out of there and in some place far more private.

Heat speared through her with the thought of how quickly they could be away from there, their clothes stripped away, limbs tangled, naked and sweaty. Those strong, very capable-looking lips of his on hers, his tongue stroking her flesh with damp, lazy licks. The hot, hard length of his shaft pushing between her thighs and deep into her sheath.

Oh, yes, she wanted that. Wanted to let go and just feel.

If only the circumstances were right. . . .

Jillian struggled to mask her eagerness. That he knew Mike didn't bother her. Once they returned from their honeymoon, Mike and Molly would be moving halfway across the country. The only things that mattered here were that she wouldn't be seeing or hearing from this man after tonight and that her actions with him couldn't return to harm her. "Where are you from?"

The slow movement of his thumb along the underside of her breast paused, starting again with his reply. "Chicago."

Anticipation jetted through her, pushing her building desire to new heights. He wasn't from around here, and the more she looked at him, the more certain she was they'd never met. Those two factors combined were an even greater stimulant than his potent grin. They meant the circumstances were right. And that meant she was going to have the one thing she'd craved these last four years even more than the loud, slightly tacky outfits that used to make up her wardrobe.

She was going to have no-holds-barred, kill the composure and give into the thrill sex. Hallelujah!

"What about a name?"

She didn't bother to mask her eagerness and he clearly took note. His penis jerked against her belly and his expression became one of urgency. "Brendan," he said, the calm tone belying his hot look.

"Just Brendan?"

"That would all depend. Is it just Jilly?"

Jillian managed to stop herself from correcting his usage of her childhood name. It was immature and completely removed from the capable, commanding woman she'd transformed herself into. But, for tonight, it was perfect.

Smiling, she moved her hands from his neck to coast over his sides. She thanked the glasses of wine she'd had with dinner, and moved her hands lower still. Her fingers reached his tuxedo pants and, through the thin material of his dress shirt, she caressed the virile flesh just above his waist.

His breath rushed in and his cock jerked once again.

Her smile growing with the distinctly female power that assailed her, she brought her lips to his ear. The spicy tang of aftershave and something far more intoxicating filled her senses as she whispered, "Just Jilly, and so you don't have to waste your time asking, the answer is yes."

For a second or two when Jilly had swiveled around and stared up into his eyes, her own filled with desire as much as what appeared to be hesitancy, Brendan had thought he'd made a mistake—that she wasn't the hot-blooded vixen her invigorating dance moves, and the bold way she'd ground her mound against his hand in a room full of people, seemed to indicate. Then her cautious look had faded and she'd snaked her palms down his chest and breathed one very warm and willing yes into his ear.

Coincidentally, it was the same word leaving her lips now, as they stood twined together inside his hotel suite's doorway. They hadn't made it any farther.

He leaned into the softness of her body and ran his tongue over the spot on her neck where her pulse beat erratically. Her hands buried in his hair, short nails biting with just enough pressure to have the blood screaming to life in his veins.

Jilly squirmed, and the hard ridge of her pubic bone brushed over his rigid shaft. Shuddering with the need the simple caress brought forth, he turned his teasing licks to fervent nips.

She shivered in his arms and tossed her head back. "Oh, yes. Yes. Yes!"

Brendan stopped his nibbling to grin at that last ecstatic one. If she made this much noise when all they'd manage to accomplish so far was a little necking, what would she be like when they got around to the main event? Not that he was complaining. He happened to be a big fan of a woman who wasn't afraid to let her love for sex show.

She lifted her head and met his gaze. Her hands moved to cup his ass. She tugged him closer yet and rotated her pelvis against his. "I want you, Brendan. I want you now. Right now!"

Had he actually thought her the cautious type for a second or two back downstairs? Fuck, no, nothing cautious about this one. She was all fire and impatience. And sex, he added with a short laugh he let flow into his words. "Now? No patience, sweetheart? No buildup? Just get to it?"

"I had my buildup on the dance floor. I don't need more."

"What if I do?"

Wariness flashed through her moss-green eyes, then was gone as one of her hands released his buttocks to cup his dick through his pants. An impish smile curved her lips. "I can feel. You don't need any more buildup, either."

Jilly's fingers clasped tighter, pumping his stiff cock. He groaned. If she kept up with the squeezing, he also wouldn't need to bother with taking his clothes off or locating a condom. He'd be coming right here by the suite's entrance.

Not that it was a bad idea. In fact, it was a very good idea.

Moving too fast to allow her the time to digest his actions, Brendan jerked from her hold and slid his hands down the front of her dress and under the short hem. Elation filled him as his fingers met with the crotch of her panties, making it clear she wore the type of stockings that were hooked to a garter belt and ended at the tops of her thighs.

He pushed past the damp lace and speared through the curls beneath to finger her slit. With a shallow gasp, Jilly released a hot stream of breath into his face. He liked the sound of that, of her losing control. From the way she'd taken over their sensual dancing to her agreement to have sex even before he could ask, he took her as the type who had to be on top and in command, both in bed and in every other facet of life. It was time she learned change could be a good thing. "You're wet."

"Yes."

"But not enough."

"What?"

He moved his finger, stroking the swollen lips of her juicy cunt, but going no farther. He wanted to build this up the way she said she didn't need. He wanted to make her come undone completely, until she was thrashing in his arms and screaming with her climax.

Her breathing grew shallower with each caress of her pussy lips and finally he allowed himself to go farther, to rub at her engorged clit. She shuddered with that first touch and his entire body vibrated with the unguarded look on her face.

Damn, she was stunning when she let herself go. Not more stunning than other women he'd fucked, just different, that something different that had convinced him to break from the norm and be the one to do the approaching.

Brendan stilled his teasing and skewered one finger deep inside her warm, slick sheath. Her eyes flared wide and then shut.

"Open them, Jilly!" In the past he'd never cared about watching the excitement in his lover's eyes—only pleasing their bodies. This woman he wanted to feel and see everything with. Maybe it was because she didn't seem to recognize him and want him for his money or legacy, the way so many others did, or maybe it was something else. It was a maybe he'd ponder later; right now there were far more pressing matters at hand.

Jilly opened her eyes. He added another finger to the first, plunging in and out of her drenched cunt, rubbing against her clit with each deep thrust. He reveled in every whimper, every throaty sigh, and the awe of rapture building on her expressive face. "I want to watch your eyes when you come. And you will come. You want to right now. I can feel your pussy contracting, begging to be let free. Come for me, Jilly. Let go."

"Not like . . ." The muscles of her sex compressed, pulling at his fingers, hardening his cock to the point of explosion. "Wasn't . . . supposed to . . . be like . . ." Her eyes slammed shut. She snapped them open again as her pussy clenched around him, contracting tighter, tighter, then all at once letting go. "Oh, God. . . ."

Hot cream poured over his fingers, showering his palm and forcing him to mentally stop himself from responding in kind. This moment was for her. There was plenty of time for him later. "That's it, sweetheart. Just let go."

Brendan pulled free of her sex and brushed his fingers across her clit. Jilly's body let loose with another round of tremors. She bit down on her lower lip and her cheeks blazed with vivid pink. Her eyes stayed focused on his. Focused and so damned green and direct they seemed to see right through him.

"Fuck, you're so intense. I love watching your face when you come. It makes me want to see how many different expressions I can bring out. How you'll look when I take you with my mouth, my tongue. When I fill up your sweet cunt from behind. I want to see it all, Jilly, but I don't think one night will give us enough time.

"Once I move here permanently, we'll meet again. Wherever you want. Once more, or twice. However long it takes to see—"

A squeak slipped past her parted lips, cutting him off short. She closed her mouth and took a step to her left, dislodging his fingers from her body. Her head whipped around, coming to a stop facing the opposite wall. "Oh, my God, would you look at the time! Ten forty-five already."

"Like I said, we won't have time for everything tonight, but we'll still have time for plenty."

Jilly continued to stare at the wall clock another few seconds and then looked back at him. Determination filled eyes that moments ago had been dark with ecstasy. "No. We don't. I—I have to go. Now!"

"What?" Brendan took a step back. Was she fucking kidding him? Things were just getting good and she had to go?

"I was supposed to be home by ten."

Yeah, she had to be kidding him. Who in their right mind went to a wedding reception with the intention of leaving by ten o'clock? A kid, or maybe a ninety-year-old. Neither of which she happened to be.

Feeling irritation made all the worse by the restless ache in his pants, he smirked at her. "And this is because of your Cinderella complex?"

She frowned. "She could stay out until midnight."

He almost laughed with the irony in the remark, only he

wasn't up to laughter at the moment. "My point exactly. What the hell's the rush? Mommy and Daddy have the curfew reins held extra tightly tonight?"

Fine lines marred Jilly's forehead. She wrapped her arms around her waist and stared at him like she'd just reentered her body and didn't like what the person who'd taken over in her absence had done. Unfolding her arms, she moved to the door. "I—I'm sorry. I have to go. Ginger needs me."

"Ginger?" As in her daughter, maybe?

"My . . . she just needs me." She opened the door and slipped through to the other side, closing it behind her.

Brendan stared at the door, uncertain of what he was feeling. Shock. Anger. Disbelief. Maybe a combination of them, all over the unlikelihood of what had just happened.

Women never walked out on him. Sure as hell not without a good-bye or an explanation to their abrupt departure. And for damned sure not seconds after he'd given them an orgasm with the intention of supplying several more. But then, women generally knew who he was. Jilly hadn't and she'd wanted him all the same, at least for a small amount of time. That made her one among the masses. Having left him with a major hard-on or not, it also made her a challenge he couldn't resist, not when he'd yet to taste that slightly too-wide mouth of hers.

"You left to feed your dog, and that doesn't strike you as odd behavior?"

Jillian frowned at her friend Tawny, who sat next to her in the boardroom, waiting for the Monday morning meeting to start. They were keeping their voices lowered, but she was still far from comfortable talking about her personal life around her coworkers. "I knew she'd be hungry. I always feed her before I go to bed and I always go—"

"To bed at ten thirty," Tawny finished with a knowing look. "That you live by a hard-and-fast schedule these days is clear. What's also clear is that your leaving had nothing to do with a schedule, but the fact that you were scared."

"What?" The word came out loudly. She cast a surreptitious glance around, thankful to find no one paying attention.

"You were afraid of letting go enough to have a little fun."

"I have plenty of fun and I wasn't scared."

"Uh-huh, right. The hard-nosed persona and black-widow wardrobe might have the rest of these people convinced, but, girl, I know you better. I know the real you. I also know that outside of your brief lapse Saturday night, the last time you let the real you come out to play was four years ago when we got drunk off Jell-O shots at the company New Year's party."

And Jillian had subsequently proceeded to ring in the New Year by kissing every guy in the place on the mouth whether he was single or not. Every guy including the husband of a major hotel chain proprietor with whom she'd been in the throes of signing a grand-scale deal. The deal had gone belly-up fifteen minutes later and the job Jillian loved had come damned close to going right along with it.

Heat raced into her cheeks with the far-from-pleasant memory and she focused on her portfolio on the table in front of her. She wasn't afraid of letting go of the cool and composed professional image she'd spent every day establishing since that fateful night. But she also wouldn't screw it up. She'd worked too hard to get here, on the cusp of taking over the role as senior advertising account executive when Donaldson retired next month, to jeopardize things over one night of fun—even if the mere thought of the fun currently under discussion had her sex growing moist and tingly, and her pulse picking up.

She pushed the sensations aside and glanced at her friend. "Fine, I'm not exactly the life of the party on a routine basis. I lived that life once. I don't want it anymore."

Tawny's hot-pink lips curved upward, and amusement glimmered in her eyes. "Kinda like the way you didn't want Brendan Saturday night?"

"I never said I didn't want him. I just . . . didn't have time."

"Right. Because you had to rush home to feed Ginger."

"Because I don't have time to deal with a relationship." Jillian just managed to hold back her laugh. The last thing an admitted bad boy like Brendan had been after was a commitment. He'd suggested they meet for another night or two of sex. She was well aware that was all it ever would have been.

Tawny tipped back in her chair and frowned. "If it's one night of fun you're after, then you missed your chance. By the sounds of things, this Brendan guy wasn't after anything more than a few minutes of exploration time in your pants. That being the case, it brings us back to my original point. The only reason you didn't finish what was started on that dance floor is because you were scared."

"For the last time, I was not—"

"Good morning, everyone." Larry Neilson, CEO of the advertising agency, entered the boardroom, his booming voice silencing her. "I'd like to kick off today's meeting by introducing you to Neilson's newest employee. Not that I think with his track record, he needs an introduction. . . ."

She was not scared. . . . Jillian continued her tirade silently while Larry droned on about the new hire. If Brendan hadn't brought up the fact that he was moving to the area, she would have gone through with things in a heartbeat. She was way overdue for some excitement of the sexual kind. Given how quickly he'd had her abandoning her better judgment and crying out her bliss as he brought her to climax, he definitely could have done the job.

Maybe Brendan was no longer a candidate to relieve the carnal hunger Jillian had been denying for too long, but there had to be plenty of others out there. She would simply find one to see to her needs for a night or two. So what if he didn't have Brendan's talented hands and sexy smile? She didn't need a man of his caliber to satisfy her. She just needed someone who was anatomically correct.

All right, so a decent face wouldn't hurt when it came to getting her heated up. She closed her eyes as that face began to take shape. Dark eyes were always good, the kind that seemed to look right through you and into your darkest, deepest, most intimate secrets. He might as well be tall and have dark hair.

Mmm . . . Nice, full, sensual mouth. A tongue that—

Tawny's elbow nudging into her side dissolved the developing face of Jillian's fantasy lover. She opened her eyes to glare at the other woman, but never made it past the man who stood twenty short feet away—the tall man grinning at her with amusement in his sinfully dark eyes. The man who had the breath wheezing from her lungs and her heart beating so hard it was liable to come out of her wide-open mouth.

Larry's spiel drew to a close. He added in an elated tone, "Everyone, give a warm welcome to our newest account specialist and a man who's already assured me he's in the running for the senior advertising account executive position once Donaldson retires, Brendan Jordan."